The Boarding School Series #5
The Tycoon's Captured Heart

Elizabeth Lennox

The Boarding School Series Introduction Stories are available as a free e-book from ElizabethLennox.com as well as other e-book retailers.

In addition, a sixth entry in the series (*His Unexpected Protégé*, a novella), will be available free as an e-book from ElizabethLennox.com as well as other e-book retailers. (Late January 2016 Release)

CONTENTS

Chapter 1

Slowly, the casket was lowered into the ground. Scarlett's handkerchief couldn't keep up with the tears, so she just allowed them to flow down her cheeks, ignoring the wetness as she tried to deal with the pain of losing the man who had become her second father.

She hated cancer! She hated the fact that it had taken yet another victim. Its merciless clutches were pulling yet another innocent, kind-hearted soul away from people who needed him.

Uncle Charles didn't deserve this! He shouldn't be dead! He should be right here next to her, next to all of them, threatening something horrible if… She had no idea what he might be saying and she was too sad, too grief-stricken to even think of something.

"Ashes to ashes, dust to dust," the minister said. She was motioned forward, handed a rose from one of the arrangements. Scarlett knew she should toss the flower onto the coffin, but she couldn't do it. She couldn't say this final goodbye.

Oh goodness! She'd thought she had said goodbye at the hospital just before he'd died but obviously, she hadn't finished.

"It's okay, love," Grayson said, his deep voice reverberating through her body with reassurance. His strong arm wrapped around her shoulders. That touch, that gentle reassurance, gave her the strength to release the flower. She watched it flutter into the hole, landing silently on the casket. Grayson's rose came next and they both moved on, allowing others to do the same. One by one, the mourners filed past, adding their flowers, their thoughts and prayers, silently saying their goodbyes.

When everyone had finally paid their respects, Scarlett stood there, surrounded by the numerous students who had been touched by this man's life as headmaster. So many people, so many lives changed because of this man's bountiful care. Uncle Charles had always been stern with discipline and demanding of excellence, but equally generous with his praise. He'd been headmaster of the boarding school for decades, constantly leading boys through a challenging and exciting time in their lives. But none were as affected as the five men who were lined up behind her.

Without Charles' intervention, she wasn't sure what might have happened to them. One was a British aristocrat, another a powerful sheik. The other three were extremely powerful in their own right. But one of them, the man with his arm around her shoulders, the man she...well, he might have ended up in prison if it hadn't been for Uncle Charles.

"You okay?" Grayson asked gently.

Scarlett looked up at Grayson, wishing she could simply lay her head against his broad, muscular chest. But that wasn't...they didn't...

She sighed. Grayson wasn't hers. Not in that way. No matter how much she might wish it.

Nodding, she accepted that this was the end of Uncle Charles' life. This was the final goodbye. Uncle Charles, the man who had dropped everything to come get her after her parent's tragic car accident, was now gone from this life.

Reaching out, she felt for Grayson's hand. She needed his strength now and he never failed to provide exactly what she needed. No matter what she asked, Grayson was always there for her. She moved slightly closer, just wanting to feel the heat emanating from his large, muscular body. Grayson's warmth and strength surrounded her cold hand, just as it always had. She wanted to lean into him, but she stood tall, trying to be strong for the others.

But as she looked around, Scarlett remembered that the other four all had their wives! Damon, Stefan, Harrison...even Malik had a beautiful wife standing beside him.

She had Grayson. Sort of.

She loved this man more than anything. She'd loved him since she was twelve years old. Maybe even longer. There had always been something about him that had drawn her to him. The other guys, yes, they were wonderful. All of them were tall, strong, powerful and wealthy. Every one of them would drop whatever was happening in his life if she needed help. But they were like her big brothers. They were big and tall and normally annoying, but also sweet and kind and shockingly generous. Oh, and she definitely needed to add that they were overly protective. To the point that they drove her nuts at times.

Grayson...he wasn't. He wasn't her brother. Not at all! He was big and tall and super powerful as well but he was...different. She didn't think of him in the same way as the others even though she'd grown up surrounded by all of them. And she could never think of the enormous brute as a brother. That special something about him called to her, made her whole body tingle with excitement whenever he stepped into a room.

Damn him! Why did he have to be so wonderful? So perfect! He was always there for her! When she was scared, she called him. When he had a success in business, she ran to him, eager to celebrate with him. When he bought a new house or penthouse apartment, she decorated it for him. She loved him. Every part of him, every emotion, every obnoxious, irritating, heavenly part of him.

But did he return those feelings? No! He thought of her as his baby sister, just like all the other guys. Well, she wasn't his baby sister! She was a grown woman with wants and needs!

From the moment Uncle Charles had revealed that he had cancer, all six of them, plus their wives now, had surrounded the man. Each of them, with their unimaginable wealth, had tried to save him, come up with a cure for the cancer that slowly taken his life away.

But none could save the dying man.

And now he was gone. His body was down in the cold earth and she wanted to scream at the injustice of it all. Grayson's hand slid under her hair, holding her head close as the grief shook her body. Well, at least she had this, she told herself.

Back at her house, Scarlett walked in and looked around, not sure what to do. She struggled to find something to say, some way to help each of these men. Damon, Harrison, Stefan and Malik all moved into the living room, holding their wives close. These men, including Grayson who stood aside, his hands in his pockets as he stared at the floor, had been like sons to Uncle Charles. The man had been the headmaster at their boarding school, had never given up on any of them even when they'd all deserved to be expelled for their constant, vicious fighting. It wasn't until Scarlett had shown up that the five of them had stopped fighting. Uncle Charles had said that Scarlett had saved their lives that day. But she'd been just five years old. She'd come from her parent's funeral and walked in to find the five of them fighting, all of them just a pile of swinging fists and flying feet. With her presence, they'd stopped the fighting. And with Scarlett's presence and the uniting force that it produced, the six of them had become best friends.

Oh, goodness, she remembered the day that they'd all graduated and gone off to college. It had been the second worst day of her life, her parent's funeral being the worst. But today ranked up higher than the day these five men had left her to go their own way.

Thankfully, the six of them, now ten with each of their wonderful wives, remained friends, coming together often to have a meal and catch up. Barely a month went by when several of them didn't get together. It used to be just a meal at a hotel or restaurant. Now that there were so many of them, the arrangements were a bit more complicated, but they all still got together as often as they could.

What was going to happen now?

She glanced over at Grayson, finding him staring right back at her. She wasn't sure what to think about that look.

And right now, she was too confused, too sad and hurt, to figure anything out.

3

"The other mourners will be here soon," she finally said, the first words spoken since the burial.

All of them nodded. "The caterers have prepared food." She took a deep breath and lifted her head. Looking into each man's eyes, she smiled. "Let's make this a celebration of his life and not..." her voice broke as she tried to speak and Grayson came over, putting his arm around her shoulders. Instantly, she felt better. "Let's not make this sad," she said even though her chin was still quivering. "Uncle Charles made a difference in so many peoples' lives. We should celebrate everything he was – not dwell on the fact that he isn't here any longer."

The men nodded their heads and Livia, Stefan's wife, stepped out of the room. She came back a moment later with a tray filled with champagne glasses and Scarlett smiled her thanks as each of them took a glass.

All of them stood in a circle, none exactly sure what to say. It was such a poignant loss and each of them experienced a deluge of emotions as they replayed memories of a man who had acted as a father to each of them, often more so than their actual blood relatives.

"To Uncle Charles," Grayson finally said and lifted his glass into the air. A mummer of agreements chimed around the group and ten glasses lifted up in a sad celebration. "To Uncle Charles," they all said, then sipped the cold, sparkling wine.

Two hours later, it was once again just the six of them. The men's wives had all gone to their hotel rooms and Scarlett was looking around at the five men, laughing at all of the stories, their memories.

This had been good, she thought, feeling better. Uncle Charles had died several days ago, and the time between then and now had been filled with decisions and arrangements to make. Although the details had given her something else to concentrate on, before Uncle Charles died, she'd been by his side constantly, holding his hand. Now, talking about all of the wonderful times she and the others had shared with Uncle Charles, she felt better. The sadness was gone, replaced by a happiness that she'd been given so much time with the wonderful man.

For the first time in several weeks, she felt as if her heart was lifted. The sadness was gone. At least for now. She knew she'd have moments in the future, moments when she would miss him again, but for now, she could breathe easier. This was good. These men had helped, Grayson's touch had helped, and talking had brought about a form of healing.

She smiled as she sipped her whiskey, impressed when the others slammed back their drinks and held their glass out for more. For a while now, there had been only laughter between them, sharing fond memories of the man who had been so much more than their headmaster. Scarlett was curled up at the end of the sofa, her shoes long gone and the tears a distant memory. At least for now.

4

"You doing okay?" Grayson asked softly. He was sitting beside her but they weren't touching even though she'd like nothing better than to crawl onto his lap and lay her head on his shoulder. He wasn't drinking as much as the others, but he could still slam them back.

"I'm okay," she told him and was surprised that she really was. They'd all had months to get used to the reality of him dying, had slowly watched him lose the unbeatable battle with cancer and now, as they all sat around the living room, there was a sense of peace. A rightness in being together.

He took her hand, squeezing it slightly. It was a silent message that he was there for her.

A moment later, Malik stood up. "We need to go. Our wives will be wondering what's happened to us." He looked at Grayson. "Can you stay and take care of Scarlett?" he asked. The four other men stood, each of them looking at Grayson as well, as if they were trying to tell him something important.

"I'll be here," he said and stood up, keeping her hand in his. "For as long as she needs."

The four others reached out and kissed Scarlett's cheek, giving her their brotherly support. It was a wonderful feeling to know that these men were there for her. There was nothing they couldn't do, she thought. They were all so powerful, so amazingly intelligent and wealthy. Each of them was a force, but put the five of them together and it was like a powerful coalition. No one messed with these men!

And she loved them all!

When the door closed on the last one, she turned to find Grayson collecting the glasses. His tie had long ago been tossed to the side, his jacket was probably over a chair somewhere which meant that she had an unfettered view of the tailored material stretching across the muscular expanse of Grayson's shoulders. He was so well put together, she thought, still leaning against the door.

Grayson felt her eyes on him and looked across the living room to where she was standing, leaning against the front door. "What?" he asked, amusement in his eyes.

Scarlett sighed, wishing she had the courage to just tell him how much she wanted him to take her into his arms and make love to her. She shivered, thinking how he could touch her gently and her mind turned to mush.

Unfortunately, he was probably dating someone again.

She laughed at that, looking up at the ceiling, thinking of how ridiculous that thought was. Grayson didn't "date". He had mistresses. He had them tucked into apartments wherever he needed them.

"What's so amusing?" he asked as he carried the glasses to her kitchen. The room had clean lines and pretty colors, reflecting the owner's preferences. As an interior designer, Grayson knew that Scarlett tried very hard to make sure that the

5

rooms reflected the owner's preferences. He should know. He'd bought many properties and allowed Scarlett the freedom to create. In every instance, she'd done an outstanding job. Most of her projects appeared in the decorating or home magazines and her business had grown exponentially in just the short amount of time that she'd been on her own.

Scarlett shook her head and glanced down at the countertop where the caterers had stacked up various serving platters and silverware. They'd provided most of the items for the reception, but she'd supplemented with a few of her own favorite pieces. Grayson didn't want to know what she was thinking though. He'd be uncomfortable if he ever knew all the fantasies starring his magnificent physique. "Nothing important. Thanks for your help cleaning up," she told him as she loaded up the dishwasher. "The caterers did most of the cleanup. Thanks for hiring them," she told him.

Scarlett turned around but she wasn't aware that Grayson had been so close. Suddenly, his muscular arms were around her waist, holding her steady and everything changed. He was here. His arms were around her. All the emotions and feelings she'd hidden from this man rose up, her mouth falling open as she realized at least a small part of her fantasy coming true. Now, if only he would…

In just her stocking feet, the top of her head didn't even come up to his chin. She stared at his neck, seeing his Adam's apple move slightly.

Looking up at him, seeing the same desire in his eyes that she was feeling, she wanted to shout at him to do something about it, to make a move.

But he pulled back, his hands slipping off of her waist.

Scarlett sighed with frustration. The moment was gone.

Someday, somehow she would build up enough courage to just walk up to him and kiss him, to show him how much she loved him.

Unfortunately, today wasn't that day.

"Go to bed," he told her, his deep voice huskier than normal. "I'll sleep in the guest room."

Scarlett gripped the edge of the countertop. "There's no need. But thank you."

Grayson saw the sadness in her eyes and reacted to it. There was no way he was letting her sleep in this house alone tonight. She was sad, exhausted, vulnerable and looking more beautiful than any woman he'd ever known in his life. "There's every need," he argued. "Go to bed, Scarlett."

Scarlett watched him for a long moment and thought she could detect a battle waging inside the man. Was she just imagining that? Or was she hoping that he was fighting the same demons, the same desire that she was battling?

In the end, she just walked out of the kitchen, bowing her head with both fatigue and frustration as she walked up the stairs.

Grayson watched the woman of his dreams, literally and figuratively, walk up the stairs, her shoulders sagging with the pain of her loss.

If he thought it would make a difference, he would take her into his arms and kiss her until she was shivering with excitement. But that was what *he* needed. Scarlett just needed a friend, someone to be there for her. She definitely didn't need a lust-filled night of sex. Sex that would take their minds off of the loss of the man they all loved very deeply.

When she turned the corner and he couldn't see her any longer, he bowed his head and tried to get a grip on this need. He'd wanted her for so long, he felt as if he was damned to eternal, unsatisfied sexual need. Every once in a while he would find a woman that he'd hoped would take his mind off of his feelings for the beautiful blond woman, but after a few weeks or, if he were lucky, a few months, he would accept that she wasn't Scarlett. So far, no woman had been able to obliterate his hunger for the slender blond with blue eyes that could look deep into a man's soul and make him want to be better.

He poured another slug of scotch and slung it back, wishing that it could help ease the need. It never did. Nothing helped. Nothing but a few weeks in a bed with that woman would help him.

And since that was out of the question, he was doomed.

"Hell," he muttered and went around the house, turning off lights and making sure the doors were locked. He glanced out through the windows and saw his bodyguards patrolling the perimeter. At least he could keep her safe, he thought. It wasn't much, but it was something.

When all the lights were turned off, he walked up the stairs, turning right and moving into the guest bedroom. It was decorated in masculine colors which soothed him. Not as much as being in her frilly bedroom might, he thought. He didn't give a damn what the bedroom looked like as long as Scarlett was curled up next to him. Or underneath him. Or on top of him.

"Hell," he said again and stepped into the bathroom, turning the water on in the shower so that it was as cold as possible. It only helped marginally. Stepping out of the shower, he dried himself off and slipped into bed.

Staring up at the ceiling, he wondered what Scarlett was doing. Was she crying? She'd buried her last relative today. It had been a long day, full of tearful remembrances as well as happy ones. It had ended well, he thought, overall. Would she still be upset?

And what the hell was going on with the other guys tonight? There had been some strange looks passing among them. He had no idea what was wrong, but they were all meeting for breakfast tomorrow. He'd demand answers as soon as he got them all alone.

Scarlett lay in bed, her eyes staring up at the ceiling and wondering what Grayson was thinking about. He was so close. What would he do if she slipped into his bed, curled up next to him? She'd decorated that bedroom with him in mind, making sure all the colors were dark and masculine, that the bed was long enough for his enormous height and that all of the toiletries were there for his convenience.

Would he find the toothbrush? And the shampoo he preferred? The only reason she knew which products he liked was because she'd stayed in his homes over the years. She'd snooped as she'd decorated his living spaces. And Scarlett had savored every detail she discovered about the man. She'd felt like a stalker, but what was a woman to do? She was so in love with the man, so proud of all he'd accomplished. He was extraordinary and no other man could compare. His features were harsh to some, but she loved that granite hard jawline, that slight dimple in his cheek that not many people saw because it was only revealed when he smiled. Unfortunately, Grayson didn't smile often. Oh, and that thick black hair, making his jaw shadowed even though he might have shaved just hours ago.

Goodness, everything about the man enticed her – from his broad shoulders to his large feet. She smiled into the darkness, wondering if the thing about feet and penis-size was true. She could feel her face flaming even in the darkness and she rolled over, groaning at the image of a naked Grayson popping into her mind. Pulling the pillow over her head, she tried very hard to keep herself from thinking about him. About all those muscles and the way he could look at her and she knew…she just knew that he was thinking about her.

Oh to be inside that man's head, she thought.

Or maybe not. She didn't want to know if he still thought of her as a little girl. She was a woman now. And she had needs like any other woman!

She should just find another man to date. A blond man, she thought. Someone short and skinny. Someone who was easy to talk to.

The complete opposite of Grayson!

Scarlett sighed and rolled onto her side, punching the pillow. That wasn't completely true and she was simply creating problems with Grayson and her relationship with him to make herself feel better. There had been many times that she and Grayson had talked for hours! Just a few months ago at Stefan's wedding, it had ended up being just the two of them talking after everyone else had gone to bed. That had been nice, she thought. All the others had their spouses and had been eager to sneak up to their suites at the hotel, but she and Grayson had been…well, they'd sort of been stuck with each other. And it had been so nice, dancing in his arms, walking down the aisle on his arm. They'd just been bridesmaid and groomsman, but she'd pretended like it was their wedding, that she'd just promised her life to his and they would live happily ever after.

She sighed again and the sound echoed throughout the room.

She wasn't ever going to get any sleep, she muttered.

Slapping the sheets back, she slipped out of bed. Listening carefully, she didn't hear anything. Noises from Grayson's room were silent now, indicating that he was asleep.

Slipping out of her room, she tiptoed down the hallway. She'd just made it to the top of the stairs when an arm swooped under her stomach, lifting her up and pressing her against the hallway wall.

"Scarlett?" Grayson snapped as soon as he realized it was her and not an intruder. "What the hell are you doing?"

Scarlett wasn't hurt but she was definitely stunned. The man wasn't wearing a shirt! And…well…she was wearing one of his!

"What are you wearing?" he demanded softly but with a definite husky quality to his voice when his eyes moved down her figure. His voice was even deeper as he said, "Hey, that's my shirt."

Darn him for the stupid monogrammed initials, she thought! "I…um…couldn't sleep. I was just going downstairs for some warm milk."

He looked down at her, not sure if he believed her or not. "Where did you get my shirt?" he asked.

He was trying very hard not to react, but her soft body felt so incredibly good against his. And he'd only paused to pull on his slacks before he came out of his bedroom to find out who was sneaking around the house. Never would he have imagined that it was Scarlett. In his shirt!

And she looked hot! Her long, slender legs were poking out the bottom and she hadn't buttoned it up high enough on top. He could see the curve of her breast, the shadow of her cleavage. Damn, she smelled good! Hell, she always smelled good.

"You couldn't sleep," he repeated, his mind trying to figure out what that really meant because the words weren't sinking in. Not with Scarlett in his arms, practically naked. And smelling better than anything he'd ever smelled before!

"I couldn't sleep," she whispered. She could feel her breasts swelling, her nipples puckering as she pressed against his hard, muscular chest. She could smell the musky, masculine scent of him and the toothpaste he'd used. His hair was still damp and…oh, that chest!

When her hands fluttered around then slowly settled onto his bare skin, she tested movement, feeling the warmth under the steel of his muscles. He was real, she thought. His skin was warm and amazing. Her fingers moved again, feeling the slight layer of dark hair and that felt even better.

She wasn't aware of her hips moving, shifting to accommodate him better. But she was desperately aware of his erection, of the way it pressed into her belly. From what she could feel, that thing about big feet…it was true!

"Grayson," she whispered his name, her body shifting once again, her fingers moving along his skin. He hadn't moved an inch except for his hands tightening on her waist.

She looked up at him, could barely see his eyes but she knew that they were a deep brown, so special and so amazing. They saw everything.

"Would you..." she hesitated, unable to say the words that would bring his head down.

Grayson heard the strange sound in her voice and his body hardened even more. Could Scarlett possibly want him as much as he wanted her? Impossible. But then her hips shifted again. He felt her fingers move lower on his chest.

All the signs were there, but he still didn't move. He didn't release her, but he didn't react to the signs that, with any other woman, would have told him to lift her into his arms and make love to her. Not Scarlett. She didn't think of him that way.

And yet, her fingers moved again. He caught the look underneath those long, dark eyelashes even in the dim light from the moon outside the window.

With a growl, he bent his head, testing the signals. He wouldn't kiss her. Not like he wanted to. But just a chaste kiss. A kiss on her cheek. A brotherly kiss, he promised.

She moved her head, catching that kiss on her lips. He didn't move for a long moment but then her lips shifted under his. He felt that. For perhaps a fraction of a moment, he didn't move, didn't even breathe. But when her lips touched his, moving underneath his, he couldn't hold back. For too long, he'd fantasized about this woman, about the way she would feel in his arms. And as he lifted her up, he realized that she felt even better.

He kissed her all the way back to his bedroom, not letting her think long enough to change her mind. This was Scarlett! And she was kissing him back! The most beautiful woman in the entire world was kissing him and he was starving for this kiss. He laid her down on his bed, still kissing her. Resting his weight on his elbows, he kissed her until he felt her shift underneath him, her legs lifting up to cradle his erection against her heat. He groaned as he reveled in that damp heat but he still wouldn't stop kissing her.

But then her hands moved against his chest and he couldn't control the raging desire. It was too much. It was so much better than all of his fantasies. She was here, in his arms and she was kissing and touching him.

With deft fingers, he tore the material away from her slender body, his hands moving down, cupping her breast. When he heard her gasp, he watched her features, making sure he didn't hurt her but his thumb moved across the pointed nipple, amazed at how perfect she was. Over and over again, he flicked that hard nubbin, his body in pain as she pressed her heat against his groin.

"Grayson!" she cried out, arching her back.

It was his signal. Lowering his head, he took that perfect breast in his mouth, sucking the sensitive flesh, almost laughing when she screamed. Her hands fisting in his hair felt great, especially when she tried to pull his head over to her other breast. He didn't mind. This one was just as perfect as the first one and he wanted all of her. Every scream she had in her, he was going to get tonight. He would make love to her more thoroughly than any man ever had. By the end of tonight, this woman wouldn't remember any man other than him.

His fingers deftly moved the white shirt further out of his way, his mind first thinking that it looked better on her than it did on him. And then he smiled as he thought it would look even better on the floor.

As he urgently parted the sides of the white shirt to reveal the beauty of her breasts, he held his breath, amazed at her perfection. The little rose tipped nipples were calling to him and he couldn't resist their need. His mouth closed over one, laving it with his tongue before nipping it with his teeth, making her gasp and moan in alternating turns. He loved the way her legs slid up his side, her soft skin making him ache to bury himself inside of her.

He should slow down, he thought as he kissed and nibbled his way down her stomach. He should savor this first time with her, make sure she felt every bit of pleasure. But those sounds she was making, they were driving him crazy. Every time he found a sensitive spot on her body, she jerked slightly, then her hands in his hair would demand that he touch that spot again.

When he finally made it to his goal, he smelled her feminine scent, his nose nudging her legs wider. He could see the light hair underneath the black lace of her underwear. She shifted slightly, silently begging him to do his worst, or best. He smiled, looking up at her. He almost laughed when she lifted her head to look down at him but he refrained, seeing the concerned look in her eyes.

A moment later, his fingers tore that beautiful lace, his eyes holding hers the whole time. Those pretty, red, rosebud lips opened up with his action but no words came out. Just another sigh when he kissed the top of her perfect mound.

And then a groan when he moved his mouth lower, finding her heat, thrilled to devour her inch by inch. He almost lost his control when he felt how wet she was, how amazingly hot. When he tasted her for the first time, he thought he'd died and gone to heaven. She was delicious! Her scent and the taste of her femininity surrounded him and he loved hearing those adorable sounds as he brought her pleasure. Her hands moved from his hair to the comforter beside her body, fisting the material in her slender fingers as her body exploded into his mouth.

He kissed his way back up her stomach, giving her a bit of time to recover even while he savored the sounds of her post-climax body. When he was at her neck, he lifted himself up over her, holding himself with his arms as he took in the flushed cheeks and her closed eyes. He wanted to see those beautiful, blue eyes but he was content to let her revel in that climax. She looked so beautiful, laying there like that with the smile on her red lips. He wanted to do that all over again. Maybe longer this time. He almost laughed at the idea, wanting to taste her again. She was better than the best whiskey, he thought to himself.

When she stretched and opened her eyes again, her smiled widened. "Wow," she whispered. "If I'd known it would be that amazing, I would have done something like this sooner."

Grayson's heart pounded in his chest with her words. Damn, he liked the sound of that. He grabbed protection quickly, then bent down and kissed her one more time even while he pressed against her softness. "Open for me, love," he coaxed, feeling her tight sheath wrap around him.

"I'm trying," she whispered. Scarlett couldn't believe how right this felt! After so many years of wondering what it would be like to make love with Grayson, she was finally experiencing all of him and it was even better than her fantasies, better than all of the stories she'd read. This was real, this was Grayson! And he was...wow, he was bigger than she'd thought possible.

Lifting her hips, she tried to adjust slightly. "Grayson," she trembled, hearing the worry in her voice even while he pressed deeper into her. She wasn't sure she could take all of him, she thought. "You're..." she wanted to say "big" but he already knew that.

"It's okay, love. Just relax and let me do the work," he told her, letting his fingers dive into her blond hair. He closed his eyes briefly when he pushed deeper, but then opened them again, needing to watch her, wanting to see her reactions as he filled her up for the first time.

When she arched her hips against him, he felt as if he could conquer the world! She fit him like a glove. Like a wet, hot glove that was made exactly for him.

"Deeper," she whispered, her hands sliding down his back to press his hips further into her. "Please, Grayson!"

He pressed deeper into her and felt something, something he'd never felt before. If he hadn't been looking into her eyes, he would have missed the slight movement of her eyes and he stilled. Had he...was she...?

"Scarlett?" he asked.

Scarlett opened her eyes and looked up into his, her eyes showing him how much she wanted him to continue. "Don't stop," she begged, biting her lower lips as she shifted her hips against him, pulling him in deeper.

"Ah hell, Scarlett. You were..." he shook his head, not finishing the sentence because he simply couldn't think of his beautiful Scarlett being hurt by his invasion. Not right now. He'd deal with that later, once he could think more rationally. Right now, she was squeezing him and he was having trouble breathing, much less thinking.

Looking down into her pretty blue eyes, he knew he had to help her somehow. "Love, just move…" he stopped when she anticipated exactly what he was going to tell her to do. He felt like roaring with the incredible feelings her slender body was giving him but couldn't stop moving long enough or take a deep enough breath.

He moved in and out, shifting his body and his hips to help her. Watching her eyes and her lips, he could anticipate what might be feeling better or not as good. But everything on her face told him that she was there, right there with him, ready to…

"Grayson!" she called out, almost a whisper but her whole body arched and he could feel her convulsing around him, making him climb over that peak himself. When the orgasm swamped him, he wasn't aware of pounding into her or, after he'd found his fulfillment, of the way he gathered her into his arms. All he knew was that this woman was the perfect mate. She was soft and perfect and…well, perfect for him.

Scarlett couldn't believe how amazing this man had made her feel. Her body was still tingling but that could have something to do with the way his fingers were trailing up and down her back. Did he have any idea of how wonderful that felt? How she wanted to just…

"Are you okay?" he asked, interrupting her latest fantasy.

Scarlett laughed and kissed his chest. "Better than okay," she told him and lifted her head up so that she could see his features. They looked harsh in the dim light. And something in his eyes, she couldn't see them very well, but they made her heart skip a beat.

He was regretting tonight! She could feel him pulling away, making space between their bodies!

"No," she told him and moved, shifting her body so that she was on top of him. So many times, she'd sat in his lap when he was comforting her or when they were roughhousing about one issue or another. Well, she'd been roughhousing. He'd simply been teasing her, annoying her or just pretending to battle with her.

This time though, she knew what to do. Climbing on top of him, she laid her body across his. She almost smiled when she heard his sharp intake of breath, thinking that was a positive sign.

"Think you could do that again?" she asked, trying to be enticing. She felt a little silly until she felt that hardness lower on her body. Oh yeah, he could definitely do this again.

"Scarlett stop it," he commanded, lifting his hands and putting them around her waist, about to lift her off of him and stop her. "You're too tender. That was your first time having sex and we can't…" he couldn't finish that sentence because she leaned over and his mind was distracted by her full breasts which were right in front of his face now.

"Can't what?" she asked, moving to kiss his forehead. And yes, he took the bait, capturing her nipple in his mouth.

His hands moved up to cup her bottom, holding her in that position.

Scarlett felt her eyes go back in her head as the desire shot through her whole body. "Not fair," she told him but moved so that he could do the same to her other breast.

When she shifted downwards, she felt that hardness. "Do you have another condom?" she begged, moving her body against his, loving the way his chest hair tickled her breasts.

"Damn straight," Grayson grumbled. He leaned over and pulled another condom out of his wallet and slipped it on. "Now what are you going to do?" he challenged.

He found out quickly. She didn't even hesitate as she pushed him into her heat. She was still warm and soft and felt so damn good, he had trouble slowing her down.

Scarlett grabbed his hands when he tried to hold her hips. "No, this time, it is my turn," she told him.

Grayson laughed, knowing that he could break her hold on his wrists easily. But he was enjoying her assertiveness too much right now. "So you think you can have your wicked way with me and I won't do anything about it, eh?" he asked.

Scarlett closed her eyes as she lifted her hips up, then pressed down against him one more time, filling herself with his body and taking control. "Um…shut up," she told him.

Grayson wanted to laugh. But damn, she felt good. His hands pulled out of her grip and moved along her waist, not hindering or helping her with whatever she wanted to do to him. She was in charge and he loved it. He never would have thought she could be this erotic but she was beautiful as she shifted against him.

He was trying to take note of how she liked to move, but the way her body was clenching against his, it was distracting. In the end, he couldn't multi-task and the way she was moving was too amazing. He'd just have to figure other things out another time.

When he felt her hands grab onto his shoulders, he couldn't hold back any longer. His hands gripped her hips and he took control, but left her on top. She seemed to like it, he liked it, why ruin something so perfect?

But when she burst into another mind-blowing climax around him again, her sweet sighs and her sexy noises accompanying her erotic movements, he couldn't hold back any longer. Shifting positions, he rolled her over so that she was once more underneath him and he pounded into her tight body, finding his own release.

A long time afterwards, she curled up against him and he felt her soft breath slow down. She fell asleep this time and Grayson wished he could do the same.

But he stared up at the ceiling, thinking about all that he'd learned about this beautiful woman that could drive him insane with need and crazy with her adorable taunts. She'd been a virgin!

Damn, it suddenly hit him. His sweet Scarlett had been a virgin and on the night after her last living relative's funeral, he'd taken that first time from her!

He should be ashamed. And in one sense, he was furious with himself. On another level, he was thrilled that he'd shared this with her.

But by the time morning sunshine was streaming through the windows, he was berating himself for not giving her what she'd needed last night. He should have just kept his hands off of her. She'd needed a hug and security. She'd needed a friend and he'd made love to her instead.

Chapter 2

Scarlett woke up the following morning and stretched. She couldn't remember ever feeling so perfectly…perfect!

Rolling over, she realized that Grayson was no longer in the bed. But she didn't mind. Jumping out of the bed, she grabbed his shirt and slipped her arms into the sleeves. She'd shower and hurry downstairs, eager to see him this morning, to feel his strong arms wrap around her once again.

Their night together had been more than she possibly could have imagined and she was thrilled that he'd felt about her the same way she felt about him. Who could have known that a man as big and powerful and amazing as Grayson could be so sweet and tender in bed? She'd always thought he would be more aggressive, more demanding.

As she was showering, she remembered that they were meeting the others for breakfast this morning. Darn it! She wanted to spend the morning with Grayson, to tell him how much last night meant to her and maybe make plans, or at least hope that he might want to repeat the episode. Maybe even repeat it right now, she thought as her body heated up just at the thought of having Grayson downstairs in her kitchen. He was probably making coffee for her. All the times they'd spent at each other's houses, he knew exactly how she liked her coffee. Funny, she thought, she'd never been up and into the kitchen before him, but she knew exactly how he took his coffee; strong and unsweetened, just like him, she thought with a silly giggle as she shut off the water and stepped out of the shower. She grabbed a towel, wishing that Grayson were here to do this with her.

Hurrying, she dressed in her favorite red dress and dried her hair so that it was a soft cloud around her shoulders. Adding a bit of lipstick and mascara and she was ready to go.

She grabbed a pair of red heels, almost running down the hallway in her urgency to see Grayson again.

"Good, you're ready," Grayson said, grabbing his jacket and tie. "We're late."

Scarlett stared at him. Where was the gentle lover of the night before? Where was the man who had held her in his arms and initiated her into the world of sensual pleasures beyond anything she'd thought possible?

And where was her coffee? He always greeted her with a cup of steaming, hot coffee and a teasing wink.

"Grayson?" she called out a moment before his hand touched the doorknob of her front door. She saw him stiffen and his shoulders sag as he accepted that they weren't getting out of this house without a conversation about last night.

"I'm sorry Scarlett," he finally said as he turned to face her. The yellow flecks in his dark eyes were almost non-existent now as his brown eyes apologized to her. As she looked up at him, she felt a sickness in her stomach. "You were upset about the funeral last night. You were grief stricken and," he sighed, running a hand over the back of his neck. "And I took advantage of you."

Her heart felt as if it was going to explode. He thought he'd taken advantage of her? Had he been there with her during everything they'd shared? If anything, she'd taken advantage of him! "You think last night was all about my grief?" she whispered, unable to accept that he really believed that.

Those hard, brown eyes looked down at her, not revealing anything he might be thinking. They never did, she thought. His eyes might glow or be hard, but she never really knew what he was thinking. "Wasn't it?" he asked, his body tense, his shoulders stiff with the tension.

She saw his "stand off" signals and couldn't believe it. He wasn't really doing this, was he? She'd heard of morning after regrets, but she'd never thought that Grayson would do this.

But he was! He was rejecting everything they'd shared last night. Impossible as it seemed, he was going to pretend that last night didn't mean as much to him as it did to her.

Toughening up, she straightened her shoulders and hid her emotions behind a blank face. "Of course," she snapped at him. "Because I'm one of those silly females who can't figure out what's going on inside her head. I misinterpreted what you were feeling too, didn't I?" she almost growled. She was so furious, so dumbfounded that he was switching gears once again. Last night had nothing to do with grief and everything to do with finally being with the man she'd loved for years. And he was sullying that! He was making her sound like a witless idiot! "Listen, buddy," she snarled, "If you think that's all last night was about, then you're an ass."

She bowed her head and looked down at her feet, her toes curling up inside her red shoes as the shame and anger swamped over her. "So yes. Let's just say that's all it was. And thank you for hurrying. You're right." She ached as she said those words and wanted to stomp on his thousand dollar loafers with her spike heel. She took a deep breath, pulling in her temper and savoring her anger. This man was an idiot! And a womanizer to boot. He was just trying to get out of the morning-after-tension by making excuses. Which was what all womanizers do when they can't escape fast enough. "We're going to be late."

With that, she stepped forward, opening the door herself and stepping into the cool morning. Lifting her head up to the morning sunshine, she prayed that she wouldn't start crying. That would make all of this so much worse!

Instead of stepping into the limousine that was waiting for Grayson and surrounded by his bodyguards, she walked over to her garage and unlocked her own car. Her little Miata roared to life and she backed out of the garage, ignoring Grayson's furious expression as he watched her zoom down the driveway. She wiggled her fingers at him before she shifted gears and sped away.

"Damn woman!" he muttered. "Let's go!" he ordered to his security team. Not for the first time did he grumble about the need for bodyguards. He hated being surrounded by all of these people. He wanted to get into a car and speed off. He wanted to race ahead of that damn woman, yank her out of the car and kiss her until she admitted that last night wasn't just about her grief.

A half hour later, when he stepped out of the vehicle at the restaurant, he looked through his sunglasses, his eyes searching out the one woman he wanted to see. The one woman he needed to make sure was okay. She'd been driving too fast and he was going to have words with her about that. Maybe he'd spank her adorable bottom for being so reckless. And for whatever the hell she'd said before she'd stormed out of her house.

Initially, he'd been too furious with himself to actually hear what she'd said to him. But as his chauffer drove through the crowded city streets, his mind went over her words. What did she mean? She'd said something about him assuming...hell, he'd been too angry with himself to actually listen.

When he approached the table, he noticed that everyone was already seated. And Scarlett was flanked by Stefan and Malik with their wives on the opposite sides of each of them. The only available chair left was on the far side of the table.

Pulling out the chair, he glared across the table at the little blond woman in the alluring red dress. Why the hell was she wearing red? She wore red too often. And she looked too damn good in it! Blonds weren't supposed to look good in red. But she did.

"What's going on?" Harrison asked, his eyes glancing back and forth between Scarlett and Grayson. "I thought you stayed at her place last night, watching out for her."

"I did," he snapped and pulled his napkin down over his lap.

Damon's eyes narrowed. "So why didn't you give her a ride?"

Grayson turned his furious eyes to the other man. "Because she…" he started to say something but Scarlett interrupted. "I'm perfectly capable of getting myself to any event. I don't need overbearing, overly protective giants who think they…" she stopped, realizing that she was revealing too much. "I'm here, safe and sound. Enough said."

Several waiters arrived at that moment, pouring coffee and telling everyone to make their way to the buffet tables whenever they were ready.

The breakfast was a complete sham, Scarlett thought as she sipped her coffee and moved the fruit and eggs around on her plate. She couldn't eat anything and she couldn't look up because that horrible, obnoxious oaf was right in front of her. She'd thought she'd been so smart about where she'd seated herself when she'd arrived, not wanting to be seated next to Grayson as she so often was when this group got together.

"I'm sorry, everyone," Scarlett said as she stood up. "I have a client meeting and I can't be late."

Grayson shook his head. "Reschedule, Scarlett. You need a few days to recover."

Scarlett ignored him. "Thank you everyone."

Grayson was furious that she would ignore him like that. He stood up and followed her, grabbing her arm when she brushed by him. "Who is this important meeting with that you can't cancel?" he demanded before she could take a step away from the table.

She turned to glare up at him. "It is Jeff Desmund, if you must know. But that's really none of your business, is it?"

Grayson's mouth tightened in fury. "Cancel it!" he snapped, wanting to roar at her for even considering that man as a client. "He's a womanizer and I don't think you should be doing business with those kinds of men."

Scarlett was stunned for a moment before she finally shook her head. "Are you kidding me? Isn't that the pot calling the kettle black?" After last night's amazing pleasure and this morning's dismissal of that pleasure, he had a lot of gall to say words like that to her!

The others at the table chuckled because each of the men had been womanizers before their women finally settled them down to blissful married life. "She has a point, Grayson," Damon commented, his arm around Sasha who punched him in the ribs, but not hard enough to hurt. "Maybe she just needs a reason not to handle that client? Want to buy another house?" The others at the table all knew that Grayson bought a condo, house, vacation place or changed his office style whenever he wanted, or needed, Scarlett close by. And she never failed to jump at the opportunity to redecorate anything he purchased. She'd done all of their residences, offices and even some of their businesses when it was interesting enough for her.

Grayson was furious. "Stay out of this," he snapped. "She can't work with that man." Turning to Scarlett, he grabbed her arm and pulled her off to the side. "What's going on? Why are you meeting a man who has dated just about every woman he comes into contact with?"

She pulled her arm out of his grip and glared up at him. Poking her finger into his chest, she said, "Don't you dare call that man a womanizer when you've dated half the female population of New York City as well as too many to count in other countries."

Scarlett hurried out of the restaurant, so furious and hurt by his attitude and his belief that he could order her around! How dare the man tell her which clients she could work with and which she needed to turn down! And damn him for telling her that she needed extra time to grieve! It was just one more signal that he thought last night was a mistake even when she considered it to be one of the most wondrous nights of her life!

She yanked the car door open and sank into the driver's seat, thinking about the previous night. And yes, Uncle Charles was gone. That hurt, but she was glad that he had finally passed away. He'd been in so much pain at the end. The cancer had gotten too deep, been too pervasive. The chemo treatments had only slowed the cancer, not stopped it.

Once in her car, she reached for the ignition button but her hand fell away. Scarlett laid her head down on the steering wheel, trying to handle the pain of Grayson's attitude and the loss of her uncle, all in such close proximity. It wasn't fair! If her uncle were alive right now, she would go to him and cry on his shoulder about how angry Grayson made her. But if he were alive, Grayson wouldn't have been at her house last night and she wouldn't have experienced heaven in his arms. Finally.

And no matter what that horrible man said, last night hadn't been a mistake! It had been wonderful! Magical, even. Goodness, she loved Grayson and last night had only made that love a physical need as well as an emotional one. She wanted Grayson to take her into his arms right now and tell her that everything was going to be okay. It might not be okay, but she would love to hear those words from him, to pretend for a few minutes that they were true.

Such was not her lot in life though. Lifting her head, she stared through the windshield, trying to figure out how she was going to get on with her day. She'd just have to push Grayson's comments aside. She would focus only on how wonderful it had been to sleep in his arms last night. She wouldn't think about his callous attitude this morning.

Chapter 3

"I need your expert advice," Scarlett announced a couple of weeks later as she sat down among the four lovely ladies, accepting a cup of tea.

Three of the four women snickered. Livia shook her head. "I doubt we're experts at anything other than getting pregnant," she commented, rubbing her slightly protruding stomach. She was three months along while Sasha was about to burst with her first child any day now, Sierra was about six months along. All eyes turned to Jina who immediately blushed.

"Guilty," she whispered as she nibbled on her fifth cookie. "Morning sickness leaves me around noon and then I can't find enough food to fill me up," she said, delicately trying to carefully brush the crumbs from her fingers onto her napkin.

Livia nodded her head while she pushed the cookies closer. "Been there. Done that. Don't ever want to deal with that again!"

Scarlett sighed. "You're all experts, obviously," she said, gesturing to all of their pregnancies. "You must be doing something right to be with the men in your lives. You're all madly in love and expecting so you qualify as experts in my book. And I don't have anyone else to turn to."

Sasha rubbed her back. "Well, I'd agree that we're all mad."

"Maybe the better term would be insane," Sierra teased and the other women laughed.

"What kind of advice do you need?" Jina asked. The men were in the other room and Malik had their daughter, Lika, as the men discussed some sort of intricate business deal they were planning or hatching or whatever it was that five genius businessmen did when they got together. Some might even consider it "planning to take over the world" and they wouldn't be completely off the mark. Those five men were brilliant at business and a menace to the global stock markets.

Scarlett considered her predicament carefully, not sure how much to reveal to these women. Her fingers trembled slightly at the thought of one of those men. The bad one. The horrible, obnoxious, truly-can't-stand-him-never-wanted-to-see-him-again one.

She shook her head slightly, trying to dismiss Grayson from her mind. He'd run out of her house after their one night together faster than she'd ever thought the huge man could move.

"I need advice on how to catch a man," she announced.

The four other women watched the beautiful blond woman's features carefully. "Is there a particular man that you want to catch?" Sierra finally asked, the same question all of them wanted to ask. She'd just gotten the words out first. And all of them knew that she was madly in love with Grayson. Was she finally going to act on her feelings?

"Yes," she replied. Looking up at each of the women who had become like sisters to her. "His name is Mark Sellers. He's an accountant who lives down the street from me. He's very nice, about three years older than me and..." she squirmed, feeling like a fraud. "Well, he's a very nice man but he is shy. And I don't know how to catch his attention and let him know that I'm interested."

Four mouths fell open simultaneously. "Mark?" Sierra said. "Sellers?" Sasha went on. The four of them looked at each other, not sure what to say. Scarlett was in love with Grayson. And what's more, Grayson was crazy in love with her. Why the two of them couldn't figure this out was a mystery to all of them.

Sasha straightened up, trying to be diplomatic about the idea. "Well, an accountant. That sounds like a very...nice man with a good occupation. Very steady," she commented. "And he's close by." She looked at Livia, trying to send her a silent message. "I don't think I'm a very good candidate to advise you, Scarlett," she said, but her eyes turned to Sierra, sending the same message. "I was married under duress and then left to wait for my husband to notice me for six years. So I have absolutely no clue on how to gain the attention of a man."

Sierra caught on. "And I doubt I could help you. I kissed Harrison at my engagement party to another man. And then he had to blackmail me into marrying him. Any advice I could give you would be pretty pathetic." She hesitated. "Livia? What about you?" she suggested, shaking her head slightly.

Livia bit her lower lip, glancing between Sierra and Scarlett, not sure what to do. "Don't look at me," she finally said. "I ran away on my wedding day. Not the best candidate either."

Jina chuckled when the eyes all turned her way. She'd only been silent because her mouth was full with another cookie. "Don't look at me," she said, her hand covered her full mouth. She swallowed quickly. "I only know how to avoid men." She patted her stomach gently. "And obviously, I can't even do that very well."

The women all laughed while Scarlett stood up and filled the cookie plate again, placing it in Jina's lap instead of on the table. "Okay, so who would know how to get a man's attention?"

"Grayson," Sasha said firmly, even adding a nod of her head for emphasis.

Scarlett choked on the sip of coffee she'd just took.

While Scarlett tried to catch her breath, Livia nodded her head as well. "Oh, I think Grayson is a perfect candidate to help you! Of all the guys, he's probably the best candidate. I mean, who knows the mentality of a single guy like a single guy?"

"And Grayson has that look about him," Sierra added, eager to add in her agreement to the plot to get those two together. Something had to happen! The two were crazy for each other and Scarlett was going in the wrong direction with this other man!

"The look that warns women off?" Scarlett snapped. Oh, this wasn't going the way she'd planned it at all. Not in any way!

The others laughed softly.

"What's so funny?" Harrison asked, leading the rest of the men into the room. They were here for dinner before they all flew out to various parts of the world once again tomorrow.

Jina stood up, hiding her plate of cookies from her husband and daughter. Not because she didn't want the two of them to know she was eating them but because they would steal them from her and she was hungry! "Scarlett needs a man-mentor. She's trying to get a guy to notice her and she wants someone who can give her advice."

Every set of eyes except for one turned to look at Grayson. Of course, he was furiously looking down at the blond-haired woman who constantly went to great lengths to drive him nuts. This conversation was just another case in point.

"We volunteered you, Grayson," Sasha announced, leaning forward slightly so that Damon could massage the tension from her lower back. She closed her eyes as his magic fingers accomplished the miraculous in amazing speed. "We told her that you knew exactly what men want and would be able to tell her how to get this guy's attention."

"What guy?" Grayson asked through clenched teeth, hoping that his smile didn't look as lethal as he felt.

"I'm not giving you his name," Scarlett interrupted before any of the ladies could offer him the information.

Grayson leaned closer, trying to intimidate her. "Why not? If I'm going to help you get this guy's attention, I should know his name, shouldn't I?"

She turned furious blue eyes up to him, looking at him for the first time since she'd arrived. "Like you'd help me in any way." She leaned back against the cushions, crossing her arms over her stomach, unaware of how the action pressed her breasts against the thin material of her silk blouse.

But Grayson was aware! He was painfully conscious of her lovely breasts pressing against that material and the way her nipples were taunting him, driving him even more crazy because he'd had his chance with her. "You know I always give you exactly what you want."

She wasn't aware of her hands fisting on her lap but the others all noticed. "You don't even know what a woman wants!" she snapped right back.

"Oh, are you saying…" he stopped and looked at the others who were avidly watching the interplay between him and Scarlett. He snapped his mouth shut, his mouth compressing into a thin, furious line. "Never mind. We'll discuss this in private."

Malik shifted his tiny daughter on his hip. "You gotta finish whatever it was that you were going to say, old man. We're all interested in what you thought she might be saying."

Harrison, Damon and Stefan all nodded in agreement. Something was going on between those two and they were sick of them sniping at each other. It had been going on for a couple of weeks now and things had almost gotten interesting with that comment.

When Grayson only glared at the men, Sierra stepped in, trying to ease the tension. "About that man-mentor help for Scarlett. What do you think Grayson? Do you think you might be able to give her some tips on how to catch this man's attention?"

"I think that's a great idea," Malik said, finding his wife's stash of cookies and stealing one, winking when she glared up at him. "Being Scarlett's mentor in finding the man of her dreams seems right up your alley, Grayson."

"It's a perfect fit," Stefan chimed in. "What's the guy's name? Do we know him?"

The others all laughed. Well, everyone but Scarlett and Grayson. Those two looked like they might just go for each other's throats.

Scarlett was the first to glance away and she uncurled her fists, laying her hands carefully on her lap. "No. I'm sorry. Grayson won't work. This requires a gentle touch. One doesn't send a bull into a china shop."

"I don't remember you complaining about my touch the last time," he snapped back at her.

Scarlett stared at the man's brown eyes. Were those yellow flecks near the center actually glowing? She wasn't sure, but he looked furious enough that it was possible.

"I'll handle it on my own," she told him and glared right back at him, not intimidated in any way by this man who thought he was all so wonderful.

Grayson just wasn't going to let it go. The idea of Scarlett, his Scarlett, in the arms of another man just made him want to punch a wall. "Like you've been doing such a great job of that so far?"

She picked up the delicate bone chine of her cup, trying very hard not to throw it across the room at him. "Like you would know! Last time we spoke, you were racing away from me."

"Last time we had a conversation, we were discussing…" he stopped and looked around, noticing that there were eight other sets of eyes that were watching and listening carefully. "We'll discuss this later." He turned to Malik, raising his eyebrows as if to say that dinner needed to speed up.

They all got the message and Malik nodded to a servant standing beside the doorway. The man immediately nodded back and opened the doors to the dining room. The others moved into the room, relieved to have a bit of the tension ease. All of them were aware of Scarlett standing up and trying to avoid Grayson. None were going to allow that to happen though. In fact, by silent agreement, they all manipulated the table seatings so that those two were seated next to each other. An occurrence that neither of them appreciated.

When the salads were brought in, Malik quickly looked over to the two that looked ready to do battle with each other, waiting to see what might happen. Sure enough, as soon as a salad was set down in front of Scarlett, she took her fork and carefully pronged each of the olives. Very carefully, as if she didn't think any of the others knew what was happening, she handed her fork to Grayson. He accepted the fork, still glaring at her, and ate all of the olives.

"Did you do that on purpose?" he asked his wife who was sitting at the other end of the table. No one else at the table understood what he was talking about, but Jina's smile brightened. "Of course! It was a test. I wasn't sure that…well, that things were still…" she shrugged.

"Still what?" Grayson asked.

Jina shook her head. Everyone else around the table shook their heads or rolled their eyes. "It's always been like that," Harrison explained to the newest member of their group. "As crazy as it seems."

"What is crazy?" Scarlett asked as she inconspicuously took Grayson's fork that held a stub of broccoli. She knew that Grayson hated broccoli and she hated olives. They'd developed a way for both of them to clear their plates over the years although no one knew what they were doing. No hostess was ever insulted because one of them didn't eat everything on their plate and neither one had to suffer through swallowing vegetables they didn't like. It was a win-win situation for all parties.

Malik shook his head, not understanding why the two of them didn't just admit they were perfect for each other.

Grayson spoke up, changing the subject since he had no clue what the others were talking about, which seemed to be happening a lot lately. "Nothing. Back to this guy you're trying to woo. What's his name?"

"You're not helping me," she told him, refusing to look at him.

Grayson sighed, accepting that this would be his penance for that one night of bliss with her in his arms. "Yes I am. I'm going to help you get this guy if he's really who you want."

Scarlett took a deep breath, briefly closing her eyes. The man she really wanted? Was he stupid? She shook her head mentally. No. Grayson definitely wasn't stupid. He was one of the smartest men she knew, present company included. Even among a group of brilliant men, she still considered Grayson to be smarter than all of them. She could be slightly biased, but she didn't care.

Which only meant that he didn't want her. She'd had her one night with him and that was all he'd wanted. She had to stop mooning over him. And she definitely had to stop dreaming about him. She was exhausted because every time she started to fall asleep, her mind replayed that night over and over in her dreams. Didn't Cinderella sing that a dream is just a wish that one's heart makes? Yeah, Disney knew what they were talking about. Her heart loved this man next to her.

As the meal progressed, the conversation around the table was lively which was normal. But Scarlett couldn't really get into the mood and sat in the chair, barely eating any of the food. She just wasn't hungry. At least, not for food anyway.

The servants took the main course away and she pushed her chair back. Excuse me for a moment," she said and stood up. She turned to leave but something inside of her, an anger she just couldn't hold back, prompted her to turn back around and punch Grayson's shoulder. She knew that it didn't hurt him. She hadn't even tried. But it still let him know that she was furious with him.

"What was that for?" he asked, glaring up at her.

Scarlett opened her mouth to respond but she just huffed a bit, unable to tell him what an absolute jerk he was, especially in front of everyone else. She could just imagine Harrison's dry British sarcasm if he knew that she was in love with Grayson. He'd tease her unmercifully! Stefan would probably kidnap her and dump her off in some beautiful house, pat her on the head and tell her that the sunshine would help her get over Grayson. Damon might take Grayson outside and a fight would start and Malik…well, one never really knew what Malik might do. He had an army at his beck and call so he was pretty dangerous.

She stared at her face in the mirror, blinking rapidly to try and stop the tears from slipping over her lashes. Her makeup would be ruined and everyone would know that she was upset. They were too protective of her.

"You're an idiot," Damon snapped.

Grayson looked across the table. "What the hell did I do?" he demanded, taking Scarlett's dessert. She wasn't going to eat it anyway. Besides, it was payback for the punch. Not that it had hurt. It was the principal though. He couldn't let her think she could get away with that.

"She's going to get you back for that," Malik commented, chuckling at the way those two continuously provoked one another. If they could simply...he sighed and shook his head. "Why don't you just..." he started to say make love to her but stopped himself. Everyone else at the table knew what the two of them should do. They all just needed to come up with a plan to get the two of them together.

Sierra stepped in at that moment. "So what are you going to teach her about luring in a man?" she asked Grayson, a mischievous twinkle to her eye.

The three other ladies leaned forward, eager to hear his reply. "I'd like to know as well," Livia commented.

Stefan grumbled. "You don't need to know anything more, love." He draped an arm around the back of her chair, pulling it closer to his own. He started to reach out and take a bite of her dessert but she quickly pulled her plate out of the way, anticipating his theft.

"Mine," she told him firmly.

Grayson watched with fascination and jealousy as Stefan slid a hand under his wife's hair. Her whole body froze at his touch and he was then able to reach across and take a bite of her decadent dessert. The whole table laughed softly and then turned back to Grayson's issue.

"I think you should give her ideas," Sierra commented. "Tell her the things that catch your eye when a woman walks by."

Sasha nodded her head. "Or what should she do when she walks into a bar? I mean, if this new guy actually goes to bars. We don't know that."

Grayson ignored all of their comments. Scarlett wasn't the "bar" kind of woman. "I'll have him investigated."

Livia pulled her husband's hand off of her neck and placed it on the table. "That's a good idea. Maybe you could find out his likes and dislikes so you can tell Scarlett."

"Oh, and be sure to tell her what turns a man off when she actually does catch his eye," Jina added. "I mean, of course she's going to catch his attention. She's beautiful and intelligent, brilliant when it comes to designing just about anything. She's what you men would call a 'prime catch', right?"

Grayson glared at each woman as she spoke, then looked to her husband, silently demanding that he get his woman under control. The look he received back from each of the men was basically, "What can I do?"

"She's not dating this ass," he commented with feeling.

Malik shook his head. "She's going to marry someone, old man. And it is going to happen quickly. It would be better if we knew who the guy was and we knew she was going to be safe with him."

Grayson shifted in his chair. Furious that they were accepting this situation. "She's not marrying this guy."

"Why not? You don't know anything about him. He might be perfect for her."

Grayson felt as if he might just punch one, or all, of his friends. They hadn't had a good brawl since...well, since Scarlett came into their lives. But right now, he was more than willing to break all of their faces, his fury was just too strong.

"I'll find all of his skeletons."

"And in the meantime, you'll help her?" Livia asked. "I mean, if this guy isn't the right one for her, then she's going to want to find another man, right? One day, she's going to fall in love with someone but she won't know how to entice him because she's..." she almost said she's been in love with Grayson for the past ten years but stopped herself. "Well, because she's beautiful, inside and out, and deserves a good man. Someone who will love her with all of his heart and soul. Someone who will hold her in his arms when she's sad and a guy she wants to turn to when she's happy."

They all stared at Grayson because that's exactly what Scarlett had with him even though neither would admit their feelings for each other. No matter what happened in Scarlett's life, Grayson was the man she turned to for all of her emotional needs. They were practically husband and wife already, just not acknowledging their feelings for one another. At least not to each other.

"I'll find her a man," he finally said.

The others all sighed with frustration. For a long moment, it had looked like Grayson was going to announce that he would be her man.

Scarlett stepped into the doorway, still fighting back tears but for a whole different reason now. "I don't need help finding a man," she explained stiffly, her hands fisted at her sides as she glared at the man she loved so painfully but wouldn't love her back. "I can find a man on my own and I don't need some arrogant ass to find him for me."

With that, she spun around on her heel and almost ran down the elaborate palace hallway to the room she'd been assigned. Locking the door, she pulled her suitcase out of the closet. She hadn't brought much because this was just an overnight stay. She was due back in New York tomorrow to meet with a new client but she would just take a flight tonight. She had to get out of here. There was no way she was going to fly back to New York with Grayson as she'd planned. She'd just get a flight out tonight and be done with the man! She couldn't believe what she'd just heard!

All of them thought she was so pathetic that she couldn't get a man? Was she that silly about the men she'd dated in the past? Okay, so none of them had been Grayson, which was really the only reason none of them had worked out. She compared every man she met to him and all of them came up short. No man had that special way of looking at her, the way that made her feel all tingly inside. And special. Yes, Grayson made her feel special and loved and cherished. When he touched her, she just wanted to curl up onto his lap and feel his arms wrap around her. No man had better arms, or a stronger chest, like Grayson.

The banging on the door was predictable.

"Scarlett, open the door," Grayson yelled.

"Go to hell," she muttered under her breath, continuing to toss her clothes into the overnight bag.

"Scarlett, I know you're in there. We're going to talk."

She whipped over to the door, so angry and it wasn't dissipating by not talking to him. When she opened it, she found a glaring Grayson on the other side. "Don't you ever walk away from me, Scarlett." And he stormed into the bedroom, slamming the door behind him.

"I'll walk away any time you're being an ass!"

He couldn't believe she was so angry with him. Wasn't he doing exactly what she wanted? She was looking for a man, he'd help her find a man! "What? All I said was that I'd help you find a man to marry!" he threw his arms up into the air, furious that she'd completely misunderstood their conversation. "Isn't that what you want?"

"Yes! But I don't want or need your help!" she poked him in the chest.

Grayson grabbed that finger poking him and twisted it around her back so that she was pressed against his chest. "You obviously do need my help. Otherwise, you'd already be married."

She started to wiggle against him, trying to get free but the feeling of his hard body against hers shocked her. Desire surged through her and all she wanted was for him to bend down and kiss her, to feel those hard, demanding lips, against hers. No man could kiss like Grayson, she thought. Every touch was an erotic caress and her eyes almost went cross-eyed just thinking about it.

"I don't need you to find me a man, Grayson," she said with absolute sincerity.

Grayson felt his body hardening with just her touch. Hell, he was pretty much semi-hard every moment he was in her company now that he knew all the secrets of her body. Oh hell, there were probably dozens of secrets he still had yet to discover and he couldn't believe she was looking for another man, thinking of giving another man rights to her perfect, beautiful body when they'd been so amazing together.

Pulling away, he released her. "Tell me this guy's name. I'll have him investigated and make sure he's good enough for you."

She stiffened with those words. "No! You're not having him investigated. And according to you, and all of those other hypocrites back in the dining room, no man is good enough for me."

He leaned down, his mind still alert to her scent. "Scarlett, what's his name?"

She crossed her arms over her chest. "No."

He looked down at her bed, realizing what she was doing. "Why are you packing? We're not leaving until tomorrow morning."

Scarlett stepped back slightly. "I'm leaving now."

His eyes narrowed. "You're not flying back without me, Scarlett."

Her chin went up with defiance. "Yes. I am." She wasn't letting Grayson push her around!

"On whose plane?" he demanded furiously. He knew the others' schedules and they weren't flying out until tomorrow either. In fact, he was the first to leave, knowing that Scarlett had to get back to meet with some damn client. If he had his way, he'd just buy her a house every couple of weeks so that she could decorate it and she'd never have to meet with another stranger again. It made his stomach clench every time she was meeting with someone new, someone who could hurt her.

"I'm flying commercial," she told him and walked towards the bathroom to get her toiletries.

Those words were like a red flag in front of a bull. She was only doing that to make him furious, and it was working! "Like hell you are!" he told her with a growl. "You'll fly back with me tomorrow morning! That's the end of this conversation, Scarlett," he told her with a glare down into her equally angry, blue eyes.

Scarlett glared back at him for a long moment before she walked into the bathroom and packed up her toiletries. That man made her so angry! She stood in the bathroom for a long moment, her makeup bag clenched to her stomach as she fought the need to either burst into tears or burst through that door and pound on his hard, muscular chest until he realized how perfect they could be together.

Why had he walked away after their one night? What had she done wrong? Why hadn't he enjoyed it as much as she had? She walked back out, her arms loaded with her makeup and shampoo.

"You can't stop me from flying out, Grayson. So just get out of my room." She dumped her toiletries into the suitcase, not caring about the disorganized mess.

Grayson wasn't budging. In fact, he moved closer. "Don't push me, Scarlett. You're not flying on a commercial flight. You won't even be able to get a flight out tonight."

She poked his chest. "Watch me!" she challenged right back.

Grayson was furious that she was acting so insulted. But he also knew her well enough to know that making commands wasn't going to get her to see reason. Trying to calm down, he ran a hand through his hair, trying to be logical about this. "Look, why are you in such an all-fired hurry to leave? Why not just hang out until tomorrow when we can fly back to New York together?"

"Because I'm leaving tonight," she told him, no explanation was necessary. She just wanted to get away from him. Needed to get away from him!

"You're not leaving here without me, Scarlett," he warned her, hands on his hips as he glared down at her.

Scarlett was so hurt by his attitude and all of that pain was coming out as anger. Fury, actually.

"And what are you going to do to stop me?" she demanded.

Grayson considered picking her up and tossing the annoying woman over his shoulder, carrying him to his own suite and locking the doors. Oh, yeah, the things he'd like to do with her in his own bed, where he knew he wouldn't be disturbed.

Unfortunately, his conscience wouldn't let him do that. Not again.

His eyes shifted. "You want that idiot down the street from you, don't you?" he asked, completely throwing her off.

Scarlett had no idea what he was talking about. "What guy?"

Grayson rolled his eyes. "The one all of the ladies were trying to get me to help you attract? The boring accountant you had your eyes on? Are you so fickle that you can't even remember the men you're supposedly in love with?"

Scarlett vaguely remembered the guy but she had been too wrapped up in Grayson's presence that Mark What's-his-name had flown out of her mind. "What about him?" she asked, still not sure she could even remember what the guy looked like.

"Do you want him or not?"

Pride was an ugly thing, she realized suddenly. "Yes," she snapped, crossing her arms over her chest, trying to protect herself from…well from this enormous, brilliant man realizing the truth. She had to hide that from him at all costs, she realized with overwhelming sadness.

"If you want him, then you'll need my help. I'll get information on him."

Her eyes widened. "You're going to spy on him?"

"Of course! I told you I was going to run a background check on him."

"You did not tell me that!" she came right back.

He shrugged one of his massive shoulders. "Perhaps it was mentioned with the others. Doesn't matter," he dismissed. "I'll get my security team working on him tonight. By the morning, I'll have more information on him."

She shifted slightly, trying to decide if she wanted the information or not. Well, she knew that she didn't care a fig for the other man. She couldn't remember if the guy was blond or dark-haired so why would she care about whatever information Grayson might dig up on the poor gent?

But then something occurred to her. If Grayson was willing to show her how to attract a man, maybe he could give her clues on how she could attract his attention? Maybe, if she did it right, she could share his bed for more than just one night. And maybe, he wouldn't be running from her bed, and from her, the following morning.

Yes, she thought quickly, her mind working frantically to come up with a better plan. She could do this. She could use this Mark guy as a ruse, a means to pick Grayson's brain on what he liked and disliked about women, why he ran from their beds so early in the morning, why he wouldn't fall in love with any of the women he'd dated so far, why he kept emotional distance from…everyone, even her now!

Oh, this was going to be perfect!

And if she got her heart broken again, well, at least, when she was ninety and surrounded by twelve cats and she was kicked out of New York City for throwing too much cat poop down the trash shoot, she would have memories of a few nights in this man's arms instead of just the one, magical, beautiful night that really wasn't a whole night.

Was she being greedy? Was she trying to get more than what she deserved? Probably.

Was she going to play the game and hope for more? Absolutely!

"Okay. Fine!" she snapped. "I'll wait until tomorrow but you have to promise me that you'll give me lessons. Personal lessons on how to attract a man. You have to tell me what you like and dislike when a woman walks into a bar or a party. You have to be open and honest about what men like and dislike about women."

He huffed a moment and she thought he was about to withdraw his offer. Her whole body tensed in fear that he wouldn't help her any longer. But then he shook his head. "I only know what I like in a woman, Scarlett. I can't tell you what all men like."

Her heart soared!

"That's good enough for me," she told him with a secret smile. The man didn't know what he was getting into, she thought with eagerness. "What time do we fly out tomorrow?"

Grayson saw her smile and knew that something was going on. Something he should be very wary of. "Nine o'clock tomorrow morning. And you're going to have to have dinner with me tomorrow night. We'll start our lessons then."

He wasn't asking. He was telling. Grayson spun around and walked out of the room, not able to stand next to her any longer with that damn bed so close. And she smelled good! The woman shouldn't smell so good! Most women wore that disgusting, cloying perfume that made him gag. Scarlett wore some flowery scent that, unfortunately, he suspected was just her.

As he walked down the long hallway, he suspected that the next few weeks were going to be brutally painful for him. And wonderful. Scarlett wanted lessons? Well she was damn well going to have to eat with him and be with him, meet him for lunches more often and, damn it, he was going to have her meet him for drinks too.

He smiled as he opened the door to his suite and pulled off his tie, tossing it onto the bed as he headed towards the bathroom and yet another cold shower. Inevitably, when he was around Scarlett now, a cold shower was necessary. Not that it did a whole lot of good, but at least it got his mind off of her breasts. Or the gentle curve of her waist. Or the golden glow of her beautiful hair.

He turned the water colder as images of his lovely woman flashed through his mind. If he played this correctly, he could even give her the worst kind of information.

No, that wouldn't be good. He wanted Scarlett to be happy. If he told her the wrong thing about attracting men, she'd never find a husband. Of all the people in this world, Scarlett deserved to get married. And she deserved kids. Or more specifically, the unborn children deserved Scarlett for a mother. She would be incredible!

It suddenly occurred to him that, while he was giving Scarlett lessons on how to attract a man, he could ask her questions on what she liked in a man.

He could change, he thought as he shut off the water. Toweling himself dry, he chuckled at all of the women over the years who had tried to change him. He'd dumped them the moment they started their efforts. But for Scarlett? Yeah, he could become someone…nice. He pictured Damon or Stefan if he told them that. They'd be laughing their fool heads off. Grayson had never been nice. He wasn't sure it was in his character. He preferred getting what he wanted and in business, that had served him extremely well. But for Scarlett, he could fake being nice.

Yeah, it was a good plan. One he'd put into action the following morning.

Chapter 4

"So what is your plan?" she asked as soon as they were in the air, leaving Sarkit and the others behind. She'd barely slept last night as she thought about different ways she might entice Grayson, discarding them as being too silly. Or things she didn't have the courage to do. Around two or three in the morning, she'd come up with the idea of simply stripping her clothes off and offering herself to him. He hadn't minded when she'd been naked in his arms the last time.

But she simply wasn't that brave. She was a wimp, actually. If she were more adventurous, maybe he wouldn't have lost interest by the following morning.

As she looked at Grayson in his leather seat, she wondered if she was brave enough for him. Maybe he needed...

He snapped his cell phone shut and looked back at her.

"My plan?" he asked, looking across the short expanse of the private plane at her. She was here, in his plane and under his protection. A surge of satisfaction shot through him. But it wasn't enough, he realized. He wanted the right to protect her all the time. He wanted her under his roof. Or whichever roof he was inhabiting for the night. He wanted her in his bed, in his arms.

Hell, he wanted her.

"Yes," she repeated, shifting uncomfortably in her chair. The look he was giving her was new and strange. She couldn't interpret those glowing, yellow sparks. "What's your plan? How are you going to teach me to catch a guy? I want good intel on what men like and dislike."

He leaned back in his chair, loosening his tie slightly. "Ah, well, that's going to take a while."

Her eyes widened. "What do you mean? Are you reneging on your promise?" she asked, anger building up inside of her as the image of all of her lovely ideas started to tumble apart.

"Oh, I'll tell you what a man wants. I can only speak from personal experience but I'll give you whatever information you want to know."

This was so different from their normal conversations. She was a bit flustered. He was sitting there in his enormous chair, looking like the cat who ate the canary.

What was going on inside that brilliant mind of his? She couldn't even fathom the depths of his mind and it was scary to contemplate.

"Personal knowledge is good enough," she said, shrugging slightly to pretend she could put personal information to general use. But she was going to use his personal information in a very personal way. Against him. To have him all for herself. If only for a few nights.

"We'll start over dinner tonight. You'll tell me what you like in the various men you've dated so far and we'll go from there."

She considered her options. It sounded fairly straightforward. "And you'll tell me what went wrong in your relationships? What the women in your past did to make you shut them out?" She wasn't sure she wanted to hear about all of them, she realized as jealousy ripped through her.

Grayson thought about her question. The simple truth was, the other women in his life hadn't been her. He'd loved her since she'd turned…hell, he had no idea when his feelings changed from protectiveness to love. It had sort of snuck up on him. One day, he was just angry because she was going off to college and growing up, and the next thing he knew, he was buying a new house so that he could be with her a bit more while she decorated the rooms for him. It was such a smooth, almost natural transition, he didn't even care why or when it had happened.

"Over dinner tonight, we'll discuss it." His phone rang at that point and he winked at her a moment before he picked it up and answered it. Her phone rang as well. She rolled her eyes at his wink and answered her own phone, pulling out her computer as she discussed budgets with one of her clients.

For the rest of the flight, they worked on their own issues, both with a computer open and cell phones going. The flight attendant provided food for the long flight, coffee and sporadic refreshments, but overall, the flight was companionable. Scarlett was relieved to have their friendship back, but she knew that it wouldn't last long. Especially if she was going to make a pass at him before this whole thing was over. And if he didn't want that move, she was going to embarrass both of them.

Better to be embarrassed for a while than to live with regret and not knowing if something could have happened between them. She was somehow going to gain the courage to make her move. Once she had enough information, she'd do it. That was a promise to herself.

When the plane landed, Scarlett thought about getting a cab to take her to her own house. But she also knew that Grayson wouldn't accept that. So instead of moving towards the taxi line, she allowed Grayson to lead her over to his limousine, ducking into the back.

When the chauffer pulled up outside of her house, he stepped out and held out his hand to assist her. She almost didn't take it, too afraid of the heat and intensely shocking feelings that shot through her body whenever they touched. But in the end, she still wanted that touch. She still needed to feel him, to know that the tension was there, even if it was only on her side for the moment.

"Thanks for the flight home," she told him, standing on the sidewalk while his chauffer pulled her bag out of the trunk. "And for the ride from the airport."

Grayson leaned forward, wanting to kiss her lips but he settled for a light kiss to her forehead. "Get some rest, finish up your work and meet me for dinner tonight. I'll pick you up at seven o'clock."

He ducked into the back seat and the chauffer pulled away. Scarlett realized two things at that moment. First of all, he hadn't given her any background information on Mark as he'd promised. And secondly, he'd almost bent down and truly kissed her!

With a silly smile on her lips, she grabbed the handle on her suitcase and walked through her front door. There was a spring to her step that she hadn't had before. And hope! Goodness there was so much hope and excitement welling up inside of her!

Chapter 5

Scarlett wore a navy blue dress that night, not willing to sacrifice another red dress like the morning after...well, that morning. Smoothing down her dress, she adjusted the collar, thinking that the dress looked elegant and formal without being too promiscuous. Slipping her feet into blue and white pumps, she felt put together and just a little quirky.

When Grayson picked her up, his eyes moved over her figure, but he didn't say a word. "Let's go," he told her, his lips compressed together.

She was hurt when he only grabbed her hand and pulled her out of her door, barely giving her time to pull her front door closed and make sure it was locked.

When they were in the limousine, she turned to him, was about to snap at him and demand to know what was wrong with him, but the grim expression on his rugged features stopped her from asking him anything. He was too rough, too angry looking right now.

But by the time they were seated at a very small, very romantic table with a bottle of red wine at his elbow, she was too irritated by his demeanor to keep her mouth shut any longer.

"Okay, what's wrong? I know you didn't lose at work. So what's wrong with you?"

He looked across the table at her. "How do you know I didn't lose something at work?"

She sighed and put her menu down beside her. "Because you never lose, Grayson. You are one of the riskiest businessmen I know. You do things in the business world that others would be too terrified to even attempt and yet, you do everything with complete calm and you never fail. You never lose when it comes to business." She lifted an eyebrow, daring him to challenge her assertion. When he remained silent, she leaned forward, crossing her arms on the table right in front of her plate. "So what's going on? Why are you in such a grumpy mood?"

He laid his own menu beside him. "You want to attract a man?" he asked sharply. He was irritated because she looked like a nun. Her blue dress covered her from her neck to a few inches below her knees. It was a dress his grandmother would wear and he was furious that she was sending the message that she didn't want him to assume anything about tonight. He got the message, loud and clear. No sex with Scarlett!

"Of course I want to attract a man," she told him. "Isn't that what tonight is all about?"

His eyes moved from her pretty blue ones to her neckline. "If you want a man, don't dress like his great aunt or his grandmother," he told her without any softening of his tone. "You look horrible."

Scarlett's mouth fell open on a gasp as her hand flew to her collar. "I just bought this dress! I thought it looked very retro!"

"It doesn't! All it does it make you look matronly. It is hideous." And he wanted to tear it off of her, burn it and refuse to believe the message she was sending to him.

Scarlett wasn't sure what to say. She looked down at her dress, thinking that she was insulted. But then why was she here tonight with Grayson? Wasn't she trying to see the world, and specifically, women, through his eyes? That was the whole point of the night, of his help.

Looking up at him, she smiled brightly. "Okay. So I won't ever wear something like this on a date. Tell me more."

His eyes narrowed on her beautiful face. "Wear your hair down. A man wants to see the woman's hair." He half expected her to pull the pins out of her hair but was disappointed when she simply nodded at his instructions.

"Okay, noted. What else?"

"Wear sexy underwear."

Scarlett's mouth opened, then closed. She felt her cheeks heat up and shook her head. "What does that have to do with anything?"

He smiled slightly. "It makes a woman walk differently. I don't know what it is," he said as his eyes moved down her figure, or whatever he could see of it from over the table, "but a man can tell when a woman is wearing sexy underwear."

The waiter arrived just at that moment and Scarlett's blush intensified. "Got it." She turned her attention to the waiter who was looking as if he hadn't heard anything odd at the table. He politely told them the specials for the day, then wrote down Scarlett's order, and then Grayson's, before slipping away to leave them in private once again.

"It isn't like the guy is going to see my underwear," she mumbled to herself.

"Good," he told her. "But that isn't the point."

"How can a man tell when she's wearing granny panties or something sexier?"

He shook his head. "It isn't the difference between granny panties or something different. I'm talking about the stuff that women buy specifically for seduction," he explained, leaning closer and holding her gaze. "I'm talking about he stuff that a woman wears when she's trying to get a man to notice all of the pecial parts of her that make a man and a woman different."

"How do you know the difference?"

He shrugged, still not releasing her gaze. "It's in the way she walks, the way he moves. It's in her eyes. There's just a sparkle there, a different look that lets a man know that he's going to be lucky that night."

She licked her lips, thinking about the bra and panty set she'd seen in a store window last week. She was getting over there to buy it tomorrow! "And what if he sn't going to get lucky?"

He chuckled. "It keeps a man guessing, doesn't it? That's part of the allure of peing a woman. She has to keep a man guessing, maintain that mystery so that he's never really sure about her."

"Is that what you like?"

He laughed slightly. "Oh, there's something nice about a sure thing, but the chase, the conquest." He nodded his head. "Yeah, that's better. Makes a man feel like he's accomplished something by winning a woman's hand."

She almost laughed at his comment. It was so typically alpha male. So like the man sitting before her.

After that, they talked in generalities and no matter how much she tried, she couldn't get him back to the subject of his likes and dislikes.

The following evening, she was right back across from him. "Better dress, by the way," he told her, his eyes skimming down her figure in a black wrap dress with a pretty, delicate gold chain around her neck. "You need different jewelry though."

Scarlett's hand flew up to her gold chain, wondering what could possibly be wrong with the necklace. "What's wrong with this one?" she demanded.

"Nothing. If you were meeting your girlfriends for drinks and girl chat. Or maybe for a client."

She leaned back, sipping her martini. She was trying to be bold and hoped that the alcohol would help. "But not when I'm trying to entice a man?"

He shook his head, sipping his scotch as he looked at her over the rim of his glass. "How did the client like that new living room you did last week?" he asked, changing the subject.

They fell into their old patterns of conversation and, on the one hand, Scarlett was relieved that they were still friends. But she was also frustrated because she had no idea how to get him to think of her as a girlfriend. She was back to being friend zoned and she was sick of it!

The next night, one more romantic restaurant but this time, she met him there, having a client meeting until the last minute. Or that was what she'd told him when he'd called to make the arrangements. In reality, she just wanted to get this whole dress thing right.

This time, she was wearing a red dress that clung to all of her curves. And instead of a simple gold chain, she'd splurged on a lariat-style necklace in shining gold that curved around her neck and then snaked down low, resting between her breasts. The dress revealed a lot more cleavage than she normally was used to revealing and she hurried into the restaurant tonight, eager to see his reaction.

When Grayson stood up, she knew that she'd gotten it right on the mark. The look in his eyes as she walked towards him gave away everything this time. Those yellow flecks were flickering in the candlelight and she smiled as she sauntered over to their table. The red, lace underwear she'd bought earlier today was making her hips sway a bit more than normal too and she loved the way his eyes traveled down her figure, unable to look away.

Grayson watched as his beautiful Scarlett approached the table and his jaw clenched with fury. Or was that lust? He wasn't sure any longer. She was gorgeous but all he wanted to do was to pull her back to his limousine and order her to dress in that matronly blue dress from three nights ago. It was safer, dammit! The other men, and most of the women, in the restaurant were staring. He could feel the lust coming from the other men and the fury from the women who were jealously watching her make her way across the room.

Even the waiter jumped up and held Scarlett's chair for her. Grayson almost punched the young kid out when he did that but instead, he simply elbowed the guy, pushing him out of the way as politely as possible under the circumstances.

When Scarlett sat down, the soft material of her dress parted on her thighs and he caught a glimpse of the lace on her stocking. He almost swore under his breath when he realized what she was doing but kept his cool.

For about five minutes.

"We're leaving," he told her.

Scarlett laughed softly and lifted her glass of wine to her lips. "I'm guessing I don't look matronly tonight?"

"Hell no," he growled. "You look…" he sighed and rubbed the bridge of his nose. "The dress is…"

Her grin widened. She wasn't aware of how sultry her glance was, but he felt that look right down to his groin. "And the necklace? Is this what you meant last night about the jewelry needing to capture a man's attention?"

Grayson's eyes moved down to the sparkling spot between her breasts. "You hit it exactly on the mark and you know it," he snapped.

Scarlett's smile brightened with that acknowledgement. "Okay, so now that I've got the dress code down, what else do I need to do to entice a man?"

Grayson stared across the table at the woman, not surprised to realize that he was fully erect, fully ready to take her right here on this table.

No, he shook his head mentally. Not on the table. He needed a large bed to thoroughly do the job. He needed to...

He needed to not think about all the things he wanted to do to her body. Shifting his mind, he looked down at the menu.

"What are you having for dinner?" he growled out.

Scarlett had no idea what she'd done to make him so angry but she wasn't going to put up with his grouchiness. Reaching across the table, she gently touched his hand. "What's wrong? What's happened to make you so grouchy?"

Grayson's teeth clenched as the extra stimulus of her hand made lust surge through him. Grinding his teeth to keep himself from pulling her into his arms, he shook his head. "I'm fine. Tell me about your day."

Scarlett pulled her hand back and tucked it onto her lap under the table, feeling foolish for even caring. She'd never thought of Grayson as moody, but the past three nights had been a challenge to get through. On the one hand, she loved being with him, trying to entice him and seeing the look in his eyes change. But on the other hand, he seemed...angrier now.

She was about to say something but the waiter interrupted them, placing their salads in front of them. Scarlett waited until the man had gone away once more before she continued.

"It's working just fine," he told her before she could start up again. He picked up his fork and devoured the dainty salad that couldn't satisfy his increasing appetite. Hell, nothing could really satisfy his appetite except a few weeks in a bed with this woman. Naked.

Actually, he'd need more than a couple of weeks. Maybe a couple of months. Or a couple of lifetimes.

Scarlett started discussing the clients she'd worked with today but kept her eyes on Grayson's eyes, trying to determine why he was so cranky. She gently questioned him about his day, trying to find out if something had gone wrong. But he was very closed-mouthed about his day. So by the time their meals arrived, they were barely speaking with each other.

She was wearing the dress! She had the necklace! She was even wearing the lingerie! Why wasn't he attracted to her? Why wasn't he suggesting that they walk out of this restaurant and find some place private to have dessert?

She sighed when the waiter took their plates away and sipped her wine, wishing he would just talk to her.

"This isn't working, is it?" she offered him with a gentle smile.

"No. So you're going to stop?" he demanded, tossing several bills onto the table. He saw one of his colleagues approaching and he damn well wasn't going to introduce Scarlett to the man! He wanted her as far away from this restaurant as possible so he didn't have to endure the other patrons twisting around to get a better look at Scarlett in that smoking-hot dress.

"Stop?" she asked in a whisper.

Hell, why did she sound so hurt now? He looked across the table into her pretty blue eyes, trying to figure out what he'd said. He'd only agreed with her! Her efforts to find a guy were wrong and…

No, they weren't wrong, he reminded himself. They were perfectly natural. He just couldn't be the man to help her do it. "Let's go," he commanded and took her arm, grabbing her pashmina and leading her out of the restaurant before the other man could wind his way through the tables to them.

They were out the door and he was able to tuck her into his limousine before the man was even halfway to them. Which was perfectly fine with him!

They were driving across town, back to her place when he glanced over at her. "What?" he demanded.

She laughed slightly. "My car is back at the restaurant," she pointed out, not sure if she should be amused, but she was. This was the man who never forgot any detail!

With a muttered curse, he lifted his phone and gave instructions to one of his guards to retrieve her car and bring it back to her house in Queens.

"He won't have a key," she told him.

He shook his head. "He has a key."

Scarlett wasn't going to ask how the guard had a key. All her life, the five men had been protecting her from the world. This was just another example. She used to get irritated with their manipulations but she'd learned over the years that they were only doing it because they cared and she'd also figured out how to get around their machinations.

When they reached her house, she stepped out but held up a hand, stopping Grayson from following her. "You don't need to walk me to my door, Grayson. Just…" she bowed her head, still confused by how she'd failed so miserably. "I'm fine," she told him and turned away.

Grayson noticed the droop in her shoulders and berated himself for hurting her. "Scarlett wait!" he called out, walking over to where she was standing on the sidewalk. "I have a…thing…tomorrow," he started out. "Could you help me?"

Scarlett's smile brightened. "Of course. What's the thing?" she asked.

"The usual ball stuff. Want me to send over a dress?" he asked her, relieved that he'd get to see her again tomorrow night even though he knew it would be sheer torture. Again.

Scarlett laughed. "Please don't. You've sent over so many dresses in the past few years that I don't have a closet to hold all of them."

Grayson looked at the house behind her. "You need a new house then. I'll have my realtor start looking for something bigger."

Scarlett shook her head, amusement gleaming in her eyes. "Don't you dare! I know how much I paid for this house, Grayson. And I know that you, or probably all five of you, paid a huge amount more for the house. The house was probably over a million dollars when you bought it a few years ago and I know that you guys sold it to me for a fraction of that amount."

Grayson didn't say a word, just slid his hands into the pockets of his slacks. He didn't need to correct her on the amount he'd paid, nor did he mention that he was the one who had bought the house. For her. And he'd damn well do it all over again if he wanted to. "You need bigger closets," was all he said.

Scarlett squared off with him. "Grayson, I love my house. You're not buying me a bigger house. This one is perfect for me."

He looked behind her, then back at her eyes. He couldn't see the color in just the light from the moon, but he knew she was trying to be firm. He also knew how to get around her stubbornness. "We'll see," he told her. He lifted his hand and chucked her on the chin. "Good night."

Scarlett glared at him for a long moment before she sighed. He would try to do it anyway. She knew he would. The look in his eyes told her that he was going to contact his real estate agent tomorrow morning and tell her to find something bigger for her. "Good night," she whispered back to him. Turning around, she pulled her cell phone out of her purse. By the time she had her front door locked, she was already texting a message to his agent, telling the woman to ignore Grayson's commands to find her something new.

Chapter 6

"You look beautiful," Grayson said as Scarlett walked towards him. The rose lace shimmered around her slender figure, making her legs look long and sexy as hell. He even loved the rose-colored strappy sandals she was wearing even though he knew they were going to kill her feet by the end of the night.

He took in the pretty design of the dress and, yep, his whole body reacted. It was subtly sexy while still trying to appear demure. Just like Scarlett herself. She seemed to be able to pull off just about any style she wore. Even that ridiculous blue dress she'd worn to dinner several nights ago had looked pretty hot. Maybe because he was imagining taking it off of her.

"You okay?" she asked.

Grayson looked away from her blue eyes. "I'm fine. Let me get you a drink," he said and took her arm, leading her towards one of the waiters passing drinks around. He grabbed two glasses of champagne, handing one to her.

"You look very handsome," she said, looking at his dark suit and silver tie.

"Thank you," he said. He should tell her that she looked beautiful, but another couple arrived at that moment. For the next two hours, they mingled, chatted with his acquaintances, he introduced her to several people and she introduced him to some of her clients. He was always impressed with the way she worked potential clients. She wasn't one of those people who handed out business cards at social events. Her design firm was simple and easy to remember, a priority in situations like this. He suspected that her charm and beauty had won her several additional clients tonight.

Scarlett was surprised when he pulled her away from an approaching group of people. "What's going on?" she asked when she felt his strong hand around her waist.

"We're dancing," he told her and moved into the throng of other couples who were moving to the beat of the live band playing some sort of soft, jazzy song.

She blinked up at him. "Yes, I'd love to dance, Grayson. Thank you for asking," she teased.

Grayson looked down into her laughing eyes and pinched her lightly. "Behave," he warned her.

Scarlett only laughed. "And if I don't?"

"Then I'll spank your adorable butt," he told her without hesitation.

Scarlett missed a beat with that threat, falling into his arms. She felt her breasts press against his chest and her heart rate picked up. "Sorry," she gasped.

Grayson didn't let her pull back. Her softness felt too wonderful against his body that was starved for any touch from her. Even an accidental touch! Not to mention, the way she was looking at him right at this moment, it was almost as if…

"We're getting out of here," he grumbled, taking her hand and leading her through the crowds. He didn't wait to say polite goodbyes to the organizers of the event, nor did he allow others to slow down his progress towards the doors. He had her hand in his and, as far as he could tell, she was racing towards the exit just as quickly as he was.

When he stepped outside, he'd already sent the message to his chauffer and the limousine was pulling up outside of the doors. He yanked open the door himself and pulled her into the dark interiors. "Get us back to my place," he ordered to the chauffer.

A moment later, he pulled Scarlett into his arms, kissing her before she could object. He tried to slow down, to savor the kiss, but she was just as ravenous as he was.

Scarlett couldn't believe that he was finally kissing her. She wouldn't stop touching him, afraid that if she stopped, he would come to his senses and not follow through on the promises his lips were giving her.

When the limousine pulled up into the underground parking lot of his building, she practically leapt out of his vehicle, too eager for him to continue kissing her.

"Scarlett?" a voice from the other side of the parking garage called out. "Is that you?"

Scarlett swung around, her eyes widening as her eyes focused on Harrison who looked like he was about to get into his own vehicle.

Grayson stepped out a moment later and her eyes slashed between the two men, horrified to be caught in the act in such a manner. She looked up to Grayson, who said a few choice curse words even as his arm slid around Scarlett's waist.

"What the hell are you doing in town, Harrison?" he demanded.

Harrison looked at the two that would normally be snapping at each other. Grayson had finally made a move? So his trip here was pointless? Perfect!

"Nothing!" Harrison replied with a chuckle. He waved to the couple and stepped into his limousine. "I'm heading off. Sorry to interrupt."

Grayson and Scarlett watched, stunned that their friend would hurry off in such a manner. But even as the black limousine drove away, Scarlett felt the change in Grayson. Their fabulous night together was at end. She just knew it!

Damn Harrison! She sighed and pressed the button to call the elevator.

"Sorry about that," Grayson gritted out. "I wasn't expecting him. I have no idea what he was doing here."

Scarlett smiled. "It's fine," she told him. But it wasn't fine! She'd finally gotten Grayson to kiss her again and the stupid interruption had cost her a night in this man's arms! She was going to yell at Harrison something awful tomorrow!

Chapter 7

Sierra squeezed her husband's hand. "Harrison, don't you have that place up in Scotland that needs renovation? Maybe a special decorator that could make the space more livable?" she asked, pulling her husband's eyes back to her as she sat at the breakfast table. He had been grumbling about interrupting Scarlett and Harrison ever since his return last night and now he was staring grimly at his newspaper, not reading anything in his frustration. All of them knew that Grayson and Scarlett were meant to be together. And they all knew that he was making a muck of things.

Harrison's eyes moved over to his very pregnant wife, not sure what she was talking about. "You can't go there, love. I promise I'll get it fixed up for you but we can't visit, not quite yet."

Sierra loved her husband but he was a bit obtuse at times. Thankfully, she wasn't going to relent. Not this time. He'd told her what he'd seen yesterday evening and she was thrilled that Scarlett and Grayson were making progress. All of the ladies in their group had been trying to figure out how to get Scarlett and Grayson together. "Oh, I saw that place! It's gorgeous but you're right, it is a mess! It just needs a gentle hand to fix it up slightly, don't you think?"

Harrison shook his head. "No. We're not going there for vacation, love," he told her firmly. "We have plans already."

Sierra looked at her husband, eyes wide but the return glare caused her cheeks to turn a becoming shade of pink. "Yes, but maybe…"

"No," he replied quickly, not even letting her finish the question.

Sierra laughed, picking her husband's hand up and kissed his knuckles softly. "Oh, I think it would be a wonderful place to stay for a long weekend. It's so remote and quiet with no one around for miles and miles. Uninterrupted scenery and lots of rooms that need a lot of love and care."

Harrison shook his head, not sure why his wife wasn't listening. "It isn't safe. There were some home invasions recently in the area, not to mention a few loose rocks…." His voice tapered off as he caught his wife's meaningful glare.

And then it hit him! His glance moved to the window, not really seeing anything outside. The roses Sierra's mother had put into the garden years ago were in full bloom, but he was actually seeing in his mind the castle up in Scotland, the cozy rooms, the wide, open expanses of scenery from the castle's walkways where one could see for miles on a clear day…

Sierra knew the exact moment that her husband caught on and shifted her head to try and get him to make the phone call.

He leaned forward, chuckling at his wife's brilliance. "Actually, now that I think about it, that's not a bad idea. I could ask Scarlett if she has the time to fix up the Scotland property. She'd love it there even though it is pretty remote." He lifted his phone, dialing the number. "I should probably call Grayson first, just to make sure that he can take a bit of time off from work as well."

Sierra laughed, her eyes twinkling with excitement.

After a long conversation about some business interests both of them shared, Harrison put out the idea of his house in Scotland, just tossing out the possibility of Scarlett doing the decorating and all of the security that might be needed.

Grayson heard the words and started shaking his head. "No way. You just said it isn't safe." There was no way that Scarlett was heading off to some lonely castle where someone might hurt her. Not happening!

Harrison already knew that would be Grayson's argument. "I'll send a security team to the area. They will watch the perimeter so she will be safe." He was rewarded when Sierra moved closer to him, grabbing onto his muscular arm and kissing his shoulder, the only part of him she could reach. She laughed when he wrapped his arm around her shoulders and scooted her chair closer.

Grayson's teeth clenched as he listened to his friend, soon to be former friend, offer weak security guards to protect Scarlett. Was he insane? Definitely not adequate protection if there really were some problems in the remote neighborhood. "No. Not good enough." He glared at the wall of his office, wishing that Harrison were here so that he could punch the guy in the face for offering such a bad idea. "You'll just have to fix the problem some other way."

Harrison smothered his amusement at his friend's adamant refusal to put his woman in danger. He caught Sierra dialing another number and her muttered conversations. He instantly knew that she was calling Sasha, who would then call Livia and Jina. Reinforcements were on the way!

Harrison sent a silent thanks to his wife by squeezing her thigh. "Grayson, you haven't taken a vacation in years. Why don't you go up there with your security team and check it out. If you don't think it is safe enough for her, then I'll find another decorator."

"Designer," Grayson corrected. "She isn't a decorator. She's an interior designer."

"Right," Harrison replied. "Actually, I could probably get in there and see what's going on. Grayson, you have too much to do. I'll take care of Scarlett. If the area is too dangerous, then I'll…"

"I'll do it," Grayson snapped and wanted to shut off the phone. He glared at the wall, wishing his friend to purgatory. Exactly where he was now that Scarlett wasn't in his arms. Which she would be if it weren't for this "friend's" interruption. "Stay out of this."

With that, he ended the call and walked across his office with furious strides, unaware that his friend was already relaying the conversation with Damon in Greece, the two men furthering the plot to get the couple together finally.

"Think it will work?" Harrison asked when Sierra ended her final call to Jina, shaking his head as he laughed at how obvious things were between Grayson and Scarlett.

Sierra groaned. "I've never seen two people who were more blind."

Harrison leaned forward in his chair, his agile mind working through details and coming up with solutions to keep the two of them in that castle until they'd worked out their relationship. Finally. "I think we should get things ready. This is bound to work out!"

Harrison dialed another number and, a few moments later, all eight of them were on a conference call, going over the details.

The men continued on the conference call while the women signed off, only to call back with just the women on the line. All of them were in battle mode while they worked out the details. While the men argued about which city would be the most romantic, the ladies already had the flowers picked out and a list of music started as well as trying to figure out which designer was Scarlett's favorite so her wedding dress could be started.

Chapter 8

"I've always loved this country," Scarlett sighed to herself as she stared lovingly down at the harsh stone castle. She was standing on the stone battlements, the part of the castle that looked sturdy and strong. The walls and turrets were centuries old and needed a lot of care. It was possible that several areas of the stone where the mortar had disintegrated too much over the years would need to be replaced, but she was up for the challenge. She'd hired an architect who was already busy working on the structure to make sure the walls and roofs were strong and sturdy. A gardener was designing the gardens and all she had to do was make the interior warm and inviting. It was going to be a challenge, but she could do it.

The line of SUVs and a limousine coming up the long, winding drive startled her. Because there weren't many trees, one could see for miles on a day like today when the sun was out and the humidity was low. "Who in the world?" she asked. She couldn't see the man who stepped out of the vehicle from this distance, but she instantly knew that it was Grayson. She could tell by the way he walked, the arrogant way he scanned the area, as if he were king of all he surveyed.

She smiled as he walked into the castle, his bodyguards spreading out and moving into place. The man was arrogant and obnoxious...but she'd made the decision that she was going after him. She loved him and, after that kiss in his limousine the last time they saw each other, she suspected that he loved her. She just had to get him to admit it.

He was a tough cookie. Grayson was one of those guys that the other businessmen didn't challenge. They always came out the loser. Seeing the way he simply walked into an area, she understood why he was so feared. She smiled in anticipation of the upcoming weeks. She could do this, she told herself. He wanted her. Last week after the gala proved it. If Harrison hadn't been in the parking garage, she would have spent the whole night in Grayson's arms.

Now he was here, in "her" house and on her turf. She knew this castle, had been staying here for a couple of days to start working on the changes that were needed. She could make this work, she told herself with a confidence she didn't necessarily feel. She had to make this work!

"Uncle Charles, if you're up there, could you help me a bit?" she said to the clouds. "You know how stubborn he is. If there is any advice you can give me, or if God has any secret way to get the man to love me, please send that advice my way."

Scarlett rubbed her arms, fending off the chill as she took a deep breath and walked down the stairs towards the main part of the castle. And her man.

Grayson had gone through every room in the ridiculous, crumbling castle and Scarlett was not here. "Find her!" he snapped to his guards. "She might be hurt or in danger!"

The guards were already running around, their microphones going crazy with all of the chatter as they relayed various bits of information to each other.

Scarlett stepped into the large foyer, pressing her back against the heavy, wooden door. "Hello, Grayson," she said and smiled at his surprised expression. She heard one of the guards mumble something and suddenly, the two of them were alone. "What are you doing here?"

He crossed his arms over his massive chest. "It is too dangerous out here for you to be working here alone, Scarlett."

Her smile widened. "And you're here to make sure I'm safe? Don't you have work to do?"

He shrugged, his eyes taking in her bright, yellow capris and her slim-fitting white, silk shirt that hugged her breasts lovingly. Pulling his eyes upwards, he forced himself to concentrate on his woman. "I have one of my tech guys upstairs installing equipment so that I can work while I stay here and make sure you're safe."

She laughed softly. More evidence that he loved her. More than loved her. From previous observations with the other men in their small circle, he was protecting "his woman" as Malik would say. It was the most un-politically correct thing to say, but her five men, and this one in particular, were alpha males who stalked their territory like lions, protecting their turf. She should be offended, but she knew that his protection came with many benefits. The best of which was another night like the one they'd shared.

"So what's your time schedule?" he asked, dropping his arms and moving to one of the rooms. Looking around, he noticed several cracks in the stonework not to mention the dusty furniture that would probably be more useful to an enormous fire than to hold a human body. "You have a lot of work to do around here. This place is a mess."

Scarlett didn't take offense. Grayson could find profitable business opportunities in the strangest places but he couldn't see the beauty of a building or the potential of a room as she could. This was her area of expertise and she loved every moment of her work. "I think this place is beautiful. It has solid bones and graceful lines." She looked up at the ceiling. "It has a lot of potential."

Grayson grunted, his way of stating emphatically that he disagreed but wasn't going to hurt her feelings by contradicting her.

"I'll work in the dining room until my guy is finished upstairs."

Scarlett smiled at his retreating back, loving him even more now that he was here, thinking she needed protecting from the big, bad world. He was wrong. She could take care of herself, but it gave her a warm, loving feeling to know that he cared enough to move his office here, just to be near her. Oh, he might be using the guise of protecting her. But she suspected it was just to be close. She liked that about him, she thought.

She slowly pushed away from the old, wooden door, eager to get started and even more energized now that he was close by. She had plans for that man!

Watching him walk up the stone steps to the upper level, she couldn't seem to tear her eyes away from his firm butt or the broad shoulders that were outlined by his tailored shirt. She now knew what was underneath that fine fabric. And her mouth watered, just thinking about all of those muscles. "That is fine," she said, almost to herself, still watching him. "I'm going to stay down here and start working through my ideas for this level."

Another grunt, telling her that he didn't really care what she was doing now that he knew where she was, and then he was gone from her sight. Not for long, she thought as she moved back into the kitchen so she could retrieve her sketchpad. She and Grayson had been playing poker for the past several weeks, both trying to bluff. But he'd just showed his hand and Scarlett was playing to win now. One thing about poker, she could always beat her guys.

She stood in the middle of the room for a moment, fiddling with the next button on her silk blouse. Should she? Dare she?

She glanced through the doors of the kitchen. At the top of the stairs was a small library, apparently where Grayson was planning to set up his work area but he was in the dining room at the moment, waiting for his equipment to be set up. Spotting Grayson looking down at some papers that were already spread out over the battered, wooden table that someone had probably used in a kitchen at some point, she smiled as her plan formed in her mind. Her fingers continued to fiddle with the button on her blouse while she watched him, fascinated by the way he could focus so completely on his work. So the question of 'should she' or 'dare she' was finalized as she watched him start to write something on a piece of paper. Definitely, she thought and flipped the button open. She would even open another button on her blouse, but that might be too obvious and she wasn't sure she was that brave. Not yet.

Taking her ever-ready sketchpad and her pencil, she walked slowly into the formal living room which was right next to the previously elegant dining room. She thought of all the sexy fashion models in the magazines, the way they stood, their hips, the sexually evocative poses and she tried hard to imitate those poses.

Unfortunately, her mind became absorbed in her task and she lost her sexy-model-pose, losing herself in her imagination. Laying her sketchpad on a rickety side table, she bent over and drew several of her ideas, thinking of various ways to transform the room into something special, something cozy and warm where Harrison and Sierra could sit in front of that stone fireplace and slip away from the world.

Grayson watched Scarlett as she lost herself in the redesign of the room. She had wandered in and he'd tried unsuccessfully to keep his mind on his work, but the way she was floating around, looking at walls, then sketching something on her notebook, kept drawing his eyes away from the contracts and the e-mails he should be concentrating on.

And when she bent over, he could see her very round, very perfect bottom in her yellow carpi pants, the curved globes outlined by the soft fabric.

His eyes narrowed as she bent lower, moving about and seeming to be completely focused on her task, doing that cute lower lip biting thing or sticking one of her pencils in her mouth while she used another pencil to do something on her notebook. He had no clue what she was drawing, but whatever it was, she was completely focused on her work.

Which was exactly what he should be doing. But it didn't matter. His eyes watched her surreptitiously, following her as she shifted around the room. His eyes noticed how sexy her legs looked in her kitten heels. When she turned around and leaned over, the white silk of her blouse fluttered open, giving him an almost unfettered view of the lace of her bra.

Was there a bit more of that delectable shadow showing? Grayson looked intently at her silk blouse, wondering if he'd missed something over the past few minutes. Had that button been undone before? He wasn't sure, nor did he really care. If it had come open accidentally while she was sketching, he wasn't going to complain. Nor would he draw her attention to the blouse, not wanting her to button it up again, hiding the enticing view from his starving eyes.

His body was throbbing with need. No matter how hard he tried, he couldn't tear his eyes away from her delicious body. She was both elegant and refined while at the same time, sexual in ways he didn't want to notice.

What the hell was he thinking? This was Scarlett! He'd already mauled her once at a point when she was at her lowest. He was here to protect her, not hurt her again!

Hell, if Harrison had told any of the other guys that he'd been trying to bring Scarlett into his building, all four of them would be on his case, demanding an explanation.

When that thought came to mind, he paused. What would the others do? Maybe they would force him to marry Scarlett? That was an enticing thought and his eyes moved back to her, wondering if he should…

No. He wouldn't do that to her. He wouldn't force her to be in his life. The woman deserved happiness. But he wasn't going to leave her unprotected. If there had been home invasions, as Harrison had mentioned, his only job right now was to protect her and make sure she was getting her work done in a safe and secure environment. That's all!

Turning away, he forced his mind to focus on his work. He had to get this contract finished, he told himself.

"Excuse me, but can I grab your pen?" she asked. But she was already leaning over his shoulder, that soft silk fluttering against the side of his face and he almost groaned out loud. But he fisted his hands and resisted his need to lift her up and make love to her on this table.

When she pulled back, she left behind the soft, flowery scent of her perfume. A scent that he'd given her last Christmas, he realized. As she pulled back and that incredible scent lingered, he gritted his teeth to keep his hands on the table and not wrapping around her arms to pull her onto his lap. He'd never give her another damn bottle of perfume again, he solemnly promised himself.

Her dainty fingers closed around the pen, she scribbled something on her notebook, then placed the pen back on the wooden desk. "Thanks," she said and glided away again but made sure to "accidentally" brush her hip against his arm.

Grayson watched with growing need as she moved around the room, making notes, taking measurements, drawing something before turning once again. Was she doing this on purpose? Was she trying to entice him? To drive him crazy with lust?

Or was that just what he wanted to think? If he thought for even one moment that she knew what she was doing and understood the consequences, he would toss her over his shoulder and carry her off to his bedroom so that he could make love to her before she could even squeak out any protest.

But this was Scarlett. She was innocent of those types of machinations.

Wasn't she?

Scarlett moved into one of the cozy guest salons off of the main hallway, closing the arched door and gritting her teeth as she tried hard to overcome the lust that was surging through her after that little attempt. She'd done everything she could think of to entice him but he'd only sat behind that stupid table, pretending she wasn't even there! Why hadn't he done something? Was she wrong about his feelings for her? Was she making a fool of herself?

She had no idea but she slumped down into one of the old chairs, coughing and waving her hand in front of her face when a cloud of dust wafted up. She didn't move though, accepting this as her punishment for being so obvious about her attempts to seduce the man who didn't want to be seduced. Some people suspected him of being inhuman. As she thought about all the things she'd done in that room moments ago, she wondered if the rumors were true.

But then memories of that one night with him, and then the way he'd kissed her after the gala…

No, the man wasn't a robot. He was flesh and blood and he was here because he cared. A man couldn't kiss her like that, he couldn't make love to her as he had without some sort of feelings for her.

Maybe she was doing something wrong. She wasn't wearing anything clingy. Nor did she have the sexy underwear on or the plunging neckline with the piece of jewelry to draw his eye. But she had boobs! Why wasn't he just looking at her boobs? Other men did! She'd caught them! She'd been offended but ignored them. What did she have to do to get Grayson to look at them?!

With a sigh, she stood up and dusted off her clothes and her sketchpad, trying to clear the air so that she could focus on this room and her work. Enough silliness. She'd have to come up with a new game plan because this one obviously wasn't working very well.

For the rest of the afternoon, she worked by herself, not brave enough to go back and try to entice a man who didn't seem to want to be enticed.

She worked hard, figuring out creative, interesting ways to use the various spaces in the old castle, thinking of Sierra's favorite colors, she sketched several ideas, trying to come up with options. Sierra and Harrison could then decide what they wanted the final rooms to look like and she'd hire the contractors to get the work accomplished.

Moving from room to room, she continued to work, unaware of the afternoon sunlight fading away until Grayson walked in and took her sketchpad away. "Time for dinner," he announced with a firm voice.

Scarlett's mouth dropped open, more than ready to protest his obnoxiousness. He worked long hours, why would he try and stop her from doing the same? She was about to argue, but the look in his eyes told her that he wasn't going to allow it. "Come on," he said and grabbed her hand, pulling her towards the old kitchen. There were slightly more modern conveniences in this room, but some of the appliances would need to be updated and a plumber was already working to replace some of the older pipes. An electrician had already finished the work of installing additional and updated electrical outlets so that the modern appliances could be brought in. Thankfully, it was an extremely large space and it wouldn't need to be expanded.

When she saw all the food on the counters and simmering on the stove, she was startled. "Where did all of this come from?" She'd been prepared to have just a bowl of cereal for dinner. And breakfast, actually. She loved creating exciting places in which to eat. Creating exciting things to eat in those rooms wasn't as fun. She'd never really gotten into the whole cooking thing.

There was an opened bottle of wine with delicate, crystal glasses and a veritable feast of tangy pasta, pungent garlic bread and a delicious looking salad.

"Did you make all of this?" she asked, stunned by all the food.

Grayson laughed. "No way. I had someone bring it in," he told her and poured two glasses of rich, red wine. "Here," he handed one of the glasses to her. "Now sit down and tell me what you've dreamed up to make this sad pile of stones livable."

Scarlett laughed at his description and took a seat while he piled an enormous serving of the pasta onto her plate. She'd never be able to eat all of that, but she thought he was cute as he filled up the rest of the plate with salad and added two slices of garlic bread. Amazingly, that was only half of what he served himself, but since he was twice her size, she supposed that made sense.

"I have just started sketching out some ideas. I don't know what Sierra and Harrison want at this point but I thought about some really good ideas for making the rooms a bit more warm and cozy." She stabbed several pieces of lettuce and looked across the table at him. "What have you been working on?"

Grayson took a long swallow of the excellent red wine before answering. He wasn't exactly sure what to say because, in reality, he hadn't accomplished anything today. All his mind could focus on was the way her silk blouse moved against those perfect, beautiful breasts or those long silky legs. Every time he tried to focus on work, an image of her and those yellow slacks reared up in his mind, distracting him once again.

"I reviewed some contracts," he replied grimly.

Scarlett cringed. "That doesn't seem very exciting."

"It is very exciting," he replied, when he actually did something with the contracts, he silently added. "I prefer looking at contracts and reviewing ways to make money versus drawing something. No one would be able to figure out what I've drawn."

She laughed. "Anything that has a profit and loss spreadsheet interests you."

They discussed the various repairs that needed to happen on the castle before she could start her work. As she spoke, she realized that there weren't as many problems with the structure of the castle as she'd originally thought. "The architect thinks that he can be finished in only a couple more days."

"That soon?" Grayson asked. "I thought there were some pretty major issues with the external structure."

Scarlett shrugged. "I thought so as well. But when the architect got in here, he discovered that most of the work wasn't needed. All of the areas that Harrison thought were breaking down were actually fine. There are several cracks in the stones, but the architect explained that the weight of the stone blocks actually supported each other, making it a relatively solid structure." She shrugged and took another sip of wine. "It won't stand up to a major earthquake, but it will protect the occupants during many more winters to come. According to the man I hired. I'll check with Harrison again just to make sure he didn't want additional work done, but overall the castle is still pretty solid even after all these centuries."

Grayson finished off his meal and leaned back in the chair, filling up both of their wineglasses once more. He noticed that she had only finished off a fraction of the food that he'd served her and waited until she was finished. "So how long will it take you to finish all the work that you want to do in here?"

Scarlett looked around, her eyes glancing up at the ceiling and the walls. "Well, this kitchen needs some pretty major renovations which should take about four weeks. But that depends on how soon the cabinets and other appliances can come in that I ordered." She lifted her glass and leaned back into the chair, thinking about all the things that she wanted to do for Sierra and Harrison's beautiful castle.

"I really love this place. There's just something about the old stones and the interesting rooms that make me want to just curl up by the fireplace and read a good book."

Grayson thought of more interesting things that he'd like to do in front of a fireplace, although reading a book with this woman curled up next to him would be pretty nice. "Why don't you buy it?"

Scarlett laughed. "There is no way that I could afford this place. Besides," and she looked around once more, "I can't imagine Sierra and Harrison letting this go."

Grayson grunted and Scarlett's eyes fell onto his handsome features. "What does that sound mean?" she laughed.

He shrugged and set his wine glass down so that he could pick up the plates. Carrying them over to the sink, he started rinsing them off. "You should use more red," he told her.

Scarlett's eyes were confused. "Sierra doesn't strike me as the kind of person who would like red décor."

He turned away from her when he noticed she was bending over to brush the crumbs from the table and he could see that shadow between her breasts. That enticing shadow. "When I spoke to her, she mentioned that her favorite color was red lately. Who am I to contradict a woman?" he said and walked back to the table where Scarlett was wrapping up the rest of the food. "Just go with red, like the lady asked."

She didn't respond, but thought about asking her friend. There wasn't a single room in any of Sierra's houses that had red décor so Grayson's comment just didn't make any sense. "We'll see. I'm off to bed," she told him, looking at the muscles underneath the material of his shirt. She longed to run her fingers over his back and wondered what he would do if she tried it.

She shivered, thinking of all the ways she'd like to entice him but...

"You sleep in the nude, right?" she asked.

Grayson spun around, a soapy dish in his hand that crashed to the tile floor with her question. "What the hell, Scarlett?" he demanded angrily.

She moved over to the closet and grabbed a broom and dustpan. While she swept up the broken dish and then looked up at him, it took all of her effort to hold back the secret smile that wanted to spring to life on her lips at his reaction. "It was just a question." She moved slightly closer to him. "What's wrong with the question?" her voice turned softer. "Do you?"

Grayson pulled back, his black eyebrows moving down to her blue eyes. "None of your business, Scarlett." But damn, he wanted it to be her business. "What made you ask that kind of a question?"

He pointed towards the garbage can, silently telling her to take care of the sharp pieces.

She moved over and dumped the broken plate into the can, then turned around to face him. "I'm going to try it."

Grayson closed his eyes, praying that she wasn't talking about sleeping in the nude. Please God, don't let her say that she was sleeping without pajamas. He wasn't sure he could take that kind of an image in his mind right now. "Try what?" But he knew! Damn, he knew what she was going to say and everything inside of him clenched as he waited for her answer. His hands gripped the edge of the counter and his jaw clenched.

"I'm going to try sleeping nude. There must be something to it. I mean, you do it, other people do it. There must be something quite liberating about sleeping without any other clothing between one's skin and the sheets. Right?" she asked him, watching him carefully.

Grayson shook his head and wiped his hands on the dishtowel. "You're not sleeping nude, Scarlett," he snapped out angrily. "You'll catch a cold."

That sounded like the most ridiculous reason for her not to try it. "But you never catch a cold. In fact, you're almost never sick. Maybe that's why you sleep in the nude. It keeps you from getting sick."

"That's specious reasoning and you know it. Just wear a damn nightgown." Preferably flannel. One that buttoned up to her neck, he thought. And covered everything between, right down to her pretty toes.

The image of Scarlett in a flannel nightgown popped into his mind and he almost groaned out loud. Not even flannel could make her look unenticing.

"I'm going to put it to the test," and with that, she spun around on her heel and walked out of the kitchen.

Grayson watched, noticing her adorable bottom as it moved against the fabric of her capris. All he wanted to do was lift her up, toss her over his shoulder and make love to her. He muttered several curses under his breath as he accepted that he would get absolutely no sleep tonight. He'd be spending the evening thinking of her moving around under her sheets without a stitch of clothing on. And after their one night together, he knew exactly what she looked like without all those clothes on!

It was going to be an extremely long night.

Chapter 9

Scarlett was so angry! She hadn't slept at all last night! She'd been waiting for Grayson to come into her room and discover that she really was naked and he would be so overcome with desire that he would make love to her again. But he'd stayed away all night! It was barely even six o'clock this morning and she was tired, grumpy, angry and frustrated. Why wasn't he picking up on her signals?

She'd seen the look in his eyes when she'd said she was going to sleep in the nude. He wanted her! He wasn't immune! He wanted her and he was pulling back for some ridiculous reason!

"Slam that cup down one more time and I'm going to spank that bottom of yours," Grayson grumbled as he walked into the kitchen.

He was dressed similarly to her in a pair of well-worn jeans and a soft-looking sweater. But on him, the jeans looked amazing! His slim hips made those jeans almost edible!

Or maybe that was just her lust-induced haze she was trying to think through. She had no idea but she glared at him as he walked into the kitchen.

"Coffee?" she asked, although it sounded more like a growl than an offer.

"Yes."

He leaned against the kitchen wall, not allowing himself to get close to her. She looked all warm and mussed from sleep and he clenched his fists tightly, refusing to mess up again and grab her into his arms.

He watched as she spooned more coffee grounds into the coffee machine and then slapped the container closed. She was irritated about something, he realized. What that could possibly be, he had no idea. But he had to admit that she looked incredibly hot when she was spitting angry like this.

Needing to break the silence and figure out some way to ease the tension, she looked up at him, then back down at the coffee, trying to come up with a safe subject to discuss. "What's on your schedule today?" she asked as they both stared at the coffee coming down and slowly, painfully slowly, filling up the carafe.

He shrugged. "More of the same."

She spun around, her blue eyes on fire. For some reason, his explanation of what he would be facing today just irritated her beyond her ability to stop her snappishness. "What in the world could that possibly mean? You buy up companies that make absolutely no sense to anyone except in your mind and expect the rest of the world to know what you do, how the pieces of your enormous empire fit together. Why would you even say something like that? It sounds terse and rude. And of all the people in the world, I am the last person that you have the right to say something rude to. So just spell it out! Give me more details than the annoying 'more of the same' because, I hate to break it to you, big guy, but you are the only one that can understand how your business actually makes such an astounding profit!"

She realized that she'd ended up screaming at him, her hands flailing out wildly but she didn't care. She was so tired from lack of sleep and so angry that he hadn't come to her bed last night. She wanted to run over to him and slap his face, pound her fists against his stomach and that impossibly muscular chest and hurt him just as she was hurting now.

Grayson stared at her, not sure what was going on. During their entire relationship, never had Scarlett ever raised her voice to him. She was the calm one. She was the member of their group that was always the voice of reason. When the five guys would be throwing punches and allowing their emotions to rule, Scarlett was the tiny little woman who would step into the fray with a simple "stop" and all five men would freeze, looking at her and then bowing their heads in shame because they'd once again lost their temper.

He moved across the kitchen, aware that she was trembling for some reason. "Are you okay?" he asked gently, lifting his hand up to cradle her cheek.

Scarlett felt his rough hands and leaned into his caress. It wasn't much, but it was something and she needed this touch. She needed anything that Grayson was willing to give her. Damn the man! Why wasn't he interested in her? Why couldn't he love her as much as she loved him?!

"I'm fine," she finally said, sniffing pathetically as she pulled away from him. "Coffee is ready," she told him, turning her back on him and lifting the now-filled carafe off of the burner. She poured two cups and cringed when she took the first sip. This was his French roast and she preferred the smoother flavors of the Italian style coffees.

"This is great," he said and kissed her forehead. "Thank you."

She sighed and pushed away from the cabinet. She'd pour this brew down the sink once he was finished with his coffee. "I'm going to start working."

He grabbed her hand and pulled her back. "No. You need breakfast. You didn't eat enough for dinner last night."

Scarlett laughed. "Not enough? I ate more than twice what I should have," she told him with a chuckle.

"Then you should eat more all the time. You're too skinny." He turned and pulled out a pan, grabbing some eggs from the fridge.

His words once again sparked her temper and she considered throwing her coffee cup at his muscular back. She held onto it with both hands, refusing to resort to violence. "I do not need to gain any weight," she argued emphatically.

"You're too skinny," he said again and cracked some eggs into a mixing bowl, adding in a bit of milk and spices.

She stiffened as he whipped the eggs together. "I didn't hear any complaints the other night."

She watched as Grayson stiffened, his body frozen in place for all of five seconds before he started moving again. "Well, that was an extraordinary circumstance."

Extraordinary circumstance? Was he kidding? Was he just teasing her?

He poured the whipped eggs into a frying pan and added a few other ingredients. Scarlett stood behind him and wondered what circumstances would warrant a replay in his mind. But she didn't have the guts to ask the question.

"I'm going to work," she told him and spun around on her heel, walking out of the kitchen. She was too angry, furious actually, to listen to the man who didn't want her. She'd tried her best yesterday.

Okay, well, she'd tried her best for about a half hour before her work took over her mind. She had to admit to herself that she'd lost focus. If she was going to do this, she needed to put her whole heart and soul into it.

She shouldn't have relented when she'd gotten nervous, she thought. She should have persisted despite her fear of rejection. Maybe if she had, both of them would be sleeping in this morning instead of snapping at each other because of frustration and exhaustion. And maybe she would be drinking a pleasant cup of coffee instead of this harsh sludge that he loved so much.

Ugh, she poured her coffee down the bathroom sink, unable to drink it any longer. It was too strong and tasted burnt. She preferred the smoother tastes but she'd wanted to make Grayson happy. More fool her!

She picked up her sketch book and continued working. But her mind was only partly on her work today. She kept an eye out for where he went in the house. Yesterday, she'd gone out of her way to put herself in his path. Today, she just couldn't work up the nerve to do the same things. He hadn't approached her door last night on some flimsy excuse to see if she'd truly been sleeping in the nude, even though her mind had come up with several almost-legitimate reasons why he could have knocked on her door. He wasn't totally uncreative, she knew. He could have dreamed up some sort of excuse, couldn't he?

By midmorning, she was sick of being cooped up indoors and trying to figure out what was going through the obnoxious man's mind. She tossed her sketchpad down onto a side table and stretched before walking across the foyer.

"Where are you going?" he demanded when she walked by the dining room doorway where he'd spread out all of his papers as well as putting up several large monitors. Apparently, the small library upstairs just wasn't big enough to contain the man's genius.

She looked up into his brown eyes, wishing she had the courage to simply stand up on her tiptoes and brush her lips over his rough cheek. She realized with surprise that he hadn't taken the time to shave this morning. She couldn't remember the last time Grayson hadn't been completely clean-shaven and immaculately dressed.

She sighed and rubbed her eyes, trying to get the image of his chest hair out of her mind. Again. "I'm going for a run. I'm tired of being inside."

Grayson watched her, impressed with the way she moved and more than a little turned on. But he also didn't want her going out into the countryside alone. He remembered Harrison's comments about the home invasions in the area.

"I'll come with you," he said and put down his coffee cup. He'd changed from the strong, French roast that he preferred to Scarlett's weaker Italian brew and he hated the stuff. And what was worse, she hadn't even bothered with another cup.

He took the stairs two at a time and slammed into his room, pulling on a pair of shorts and a shirt with his running shoes. When he stepped out, she was already skipping down the stairs, ready for a long run.

Oh no, little lady he thought as his eyes followed her cute butt in the leggings and wicking shirt. "Scarlett, wait up," he called out to her.

Scarlett looked up the stairs and cringed, shaking her head as she realized what he was intending. "No way, Grayson! I'm not running with you! Your legs are much longer than mine. I can't keep up with you when we go for a run together."

He chuckled at her outraged expression but wasn't relenting. "Don't be a wimp," he told her and nudged her out the door. Her idea of a run was a good one. They hadn't had much exercise in the past couple of days and the fresh air would do both of them some good.

Besides, he had to get her out of the house because there was absolutely no way he could watch her in the house in her running spandex pants and her tight shirt. There were no secrets when she was wearing that outfit. Everything was tight against her sexy, slender figure and he was practically panting just standing in front of her. She looked hot! Any man who peered out of his window when she jogged by would want her and he was determined to protect her if she wanted to go for a run.

"Grayson!" she snapped, pulling back. "You're not coming with me! That's final!" she told him and started stretching her legs, trying to loosen up her muscles.

"Can't keep up? Are you really that much of a girl?"

That did it! "Oh, you want to race? Are you challenging me?" She couldn't believe she was actually about to accept his challenge. His legs were at least a foot longer than hers plus he was much more muscular. Maybe he didn't have the same kind of cardiovascular abilities as she did, but did she really want to put it to the test?

Yes! Some silly little impulse wanted to test her strength against his. It might be just that he was looking at her with that dare in his eyes or maybe she really wanted to see how good she was. Either way, the test was on!

She glared up at him and slipped her earplugs in, turning up the volume on her cell phone so that her music would blast out any comments he might make.

She took off running, not even bothering to stretch out her muscles, too angry with him for taunting her. She moved off, painfully aware of him right behind her. When he came up beside her, she picked up her pace, determined to be ahead of him. She'd run with him several times in the past. The last time, she'd sworn that she'd never do it again. But here she was, trying to beat the man one more time. Maybe someday she'd learn, but that day wasn't today.

He was right beside her and every few minutes, he would pick up the pace. She tried to keep her breathing even, remembering all of the tricks of running to help her keep up with him. She swung her arms out to the side, no crossing in front of her body, in and out breathing, leaning over on the hills, relaxing on the downward sides...She was dying! His pace was killing her but she wouldn't give in. She kept on running, speeding up whenever he picked up his pace. She was a glutton for punishment, she thought as they jogged through the countryside.

She kept up though!

Unfortunately, after five miles, she felt like she was going to pass out. Meanwhile, Grayson hadn't even broken a sweat.

When he started up yet another hill, she stopped, holding out her hands before falling forward, gasping for breath and hoping she didn't pass out or throw up from the exertion. "I can't!" she gasped, bending over and trying to catch her breath.

Grayson bent lower, watching the woman and admiring her bottom in the tight fitting pants. He actually had to look away because his body went into instant attention, more than ready to take her right here on the craggy rocks.

When he thought he had himself under control again, he looked back at her. "What happened to you, Scarlett? The last time we went for a run together, you were able to make it seven or eight miles before begging for mercy."

She turned her head up to look at him. She meant to glare, but it just took too much energy so she satisfied herself with a simple look. In her mind, it was a glare though. "The last time we went for a run, I'd had a full night's sleep, a good cup of coffee and we were running along the streets of Manhattan, not the hills of Scotland, up and over rocks and other things. So don't you dare tell me that I'm out of shape!"

Grayson chuckled. He definitely wouldn't utter anything so crazy as to imply that she was out of shape. There was no way he would tell her that she was out of shape. In fact, she was in perfect shape, he thought. Her shape was probably too good. Maybe if she gained about a hundred pounds, he wouldn't have this painful desire to kiss her and make love to her.

Nah, he thought. He loved the woman, not the shape. Even if she gained weight, he would still think she was beautiful. Hell, he wondered if there was anything that could ease this painful need to possess her, which had only grown more evident over the past week.

So why had he decided he could work out of a crumbling, stone castle while she finished up her work? He could have just as easily sent a whole team of bodyguards to protect her. Hell, they could have even run with her, or, at a minimum, driven behind her as she ran through the streets. Living in close confines with her definitely wasn't his best idea. But would he leave? Hell no!

He looked down at the beauty who was trying hard to pretend she was finished with her run. But he knew her better. The woman loved to exercise and loved a good, long run better than anything. "Come on, Scarlett. Suck it up. Let's keep going."

He was right, she thought. It had been only five miles and she could do better than that. She glared up at him but instead of wimping out, she turned and ran down the hill. "Fine! But I'm keeping the pace from now on. You stay behind me. Not beside me because you just keep pushing the pace harder. Got it?" And that's how they finished out the next five miles. Grayson didn't mind in the least. He followed behind her, admiring her butt as she moved in and out of the streets, up the hills, down the hills and across the fields that were blooming despite the cold weather.

When they made it back to the castle, she was practically jumping up and down with the euphoria of the endorphins rushing through her. "That was great!" she laughed, throwing her arms around his neck. "Let's do it again!"

Grayson laughed, pulling her close. "How about a shower?"

She froze, thinking that he was offering to shower with her. "Um..." Was he inviting her to share the one bathroom with him? Was a good, long run all it took to make the man give in and make love to her?

"You can go first," he told her and smacked her bottom.

She stepped out of his arms as the disappointment hit her hard, unaware of the way her nipples were pressing against the thin material of her running shirt. "Are you sure?" she asked.

Grayson had to concentrate to keep her from noticing his body's reaction to her hug. "Yes. Go ahead. I have a phone call to make."

She turned around and ran up the stone steps of the castle. Right now, there was only one bathroom in the entire castle but Scarlett had figured out how to use three of the bedrooms for bathrooms. That would reduce the bedrooms from nine to six, but in Sierra's mind, bathrooms were more important than bedrooms.

She felt one hundred percent better now that she'd exerted herself and used her muscles. Goodness, she loved to go for a long run. She didn't like running with Grayson as much, but he pushed her, made her run faster. She probably held him back from really exerting himself but she didn't care at the moment. She felt wonderful! Euphoric!

Stepping out of the bathroom after her shower, she cinched the towel tighter around her body. She was looking down at the floor so she didn't see Grayson as he was coming up the stairs until it was too late.

Or maybe it was perfect timing, she thought as she stared up into his startled eyes. "I was…" she started to say, but the words wouldn't come out correctly. Not with his large, muscular body so close to her own.

"I get it," he commented back, looking down at her. She felt his hands clench on both sides of her waist and instinctively moved closer to him. "I just…" She could feel the tension in his body, knew that he was fighting to hold back from touching her more thoroughly. And that's when she made the decision that she wasn't going to allow him to do that! Not this time!

But what could she do to encourage him? What did a woman do to seduce the man she was madly in love with?

When she didn't finish the sentence, he moved forward, slowly pressing her back against the wall. "What?" he asked softly but with that gravely edge to his voice that sent shivers racing throughout her whole body. "You were just…?"

"Going to my room," she finished weakly, her eyes moving from his brown ones down to his lips, wishing he would kiss her. She wanted to feel that fire, feel the intensity of his kiss, his hands on her body and that explosive pleasure that he'd shown her the last time.

"Why?" he demanded. His mind was telling him to back off, to let her walk by but his body, aching for so long to be with her again, wouldn't listen. His body wanted this. His body was determined to feel her softness once again.

Scarlett looked up into his hard, brown eyes, the yellow flecks on fire. She could do this! This is what she'd been wanting since he arrived! "Give me a reason not to." Her blue eyes begged him to take the initiative, to do something with her. She was in a towel for goodness sake! Couldn't he just…

Grayson's lungs inhaled a gust of air as he stared down at the blond perfection in his arms. Or almost in his arms. He wanted her. Badly! "Go to your room, Scarlett. Go before I do something we'll both regret again." And a moment later, he pushed himself away and disappeared into the bathroom.

Scarlett stared at the opposite wall, beating herself up for not just dropping the towel. But the interlude proved one thing to her befuddled mind. He was interested! He wasn't immune! He wanted to be able to resist her, but he wanted her.

She'd seen the heat in his eyes, felt the tension in his body and the way his hands fisted at her waist. Oh yes! He'd wanted her almost as badly as she wanted him!

She smiled, her fingers tightening on the towel still knotted just above her breasts. For some reason, he was fighting this attraction. With a delighted laugh, she shook her head as she headed down the hallway. Oh was he going to lose that battle, she thought and almost danced into the room she'd taken over during the renovation. She almost laughed out loud with excitement and renewed determination.

Grayson stepped into the shower, amazed that the old plumbing actually worked. As the cold water streamed down his body, he couldn't believe what he'd just done. Or almost done. Berating himself for coming onto Scarlett again, he almost slammed his fist against the tiled wall, furious for putting her into an awkward situation once more.

Washing up, he quickly dried off and then moved back to his bedroom. Pulling on jeans and a sweatshirt again, he swore to himself that he would just work and make sure that Scarlett was safe. He wouldn't push himself on her. His only purpose here was to make sure that Scarlett didn't get hurt or run into any of the criminals that Harrison had mentioned. That was it!

He stepped behind his computer and focused all of his attention on work issues, not allowing his eyes to move away from his computer.

He was successful for about three hours. Unfortunately, a conference call had him pacing through the small dining room and his eyes didn't need to be glued to a document or a computer screen. They were free to wander. And they wandered right to Scarlett who was now dressed in a new pair of leggings that hugged her body, smoothing along her adorable bottom. They moved up her figure and he loved the way the soft, cashmere sweater made her appear even softer. That cozy material made his mouth water and he knew that God was putting him into a special kind of hell because he couldn't keep his eyes off of her.

Had she worn these kinds of revealing clothes before? He hadn't always been around her when she was working. Normally, he saw her in dresses or elegant suits. But out here in the countryside, there was no need for that kind of formality.

He made a strange sound when she came into the dining room with her measuring tape and started to take down numbers. That bottom was too close, he thought. He could just reach out and run his hands over her sexy figure and...

"Grayson?" someone on the other end of the conference call prompted.

Grayson had absolutely no idea what was going on with the meeting. His entire focus was on the woman examining the walls.

Scarlett turned to look at him, her eyebrows lifted higher as she listened to the person on the other end of the conference call.

"Sorry," he snapped. "What was the question?" He didn't bother to mention that he was distracted. Everyone on the phone call knew that he'd been distracted but they had no idea what that something could be. When he glanced back at Scarlett, she was smiling up at him, her cute butt sliding onto the wooden surface of the dining room table.

His eyebrows went up again, silently asking her what she wanted.

"Grayson?" the voice called out again.

"What?" he snapped, irritated that someone was interrupting his concentration on the long legs that were crossed at very slim ankles.

There was silence on the conference call and Grayson sighed, rubbing a hand over the back of his neck. "Sorry. Let's continue this conversation tomorrow, okay?"

He didn't wait for the people on the call to agree. With the press of a button, he ended the call.

Silence reigned in the dining room for a long moment. Finally, he leaned his body forward, bracing on his outstretched arms. "What are you doing, Scarlett?" he demanded, his brown eyes heating up as he noticed the pink stealing up to her porcelain cheeks.

Scarlett bit her lower lip, lowering her lashes slightly as she considered her next words carefully. "Here's the deal," she replied softly. "I don't know why you left my house so quickly after the one night we had together," she started out. "But I was wondering if maybe…perhaps…" she took a deep breath and looked up into his burning, brown eyes. "Well, I was wondering if there might be a possibility that you'd like to repeat that night."

Grayson stood very still, his mind going over her words again and again. There was no grief this time around, she hadn't been drinking any alcohol, she hadn't just buried a relative and she hadn't just spent hours at a tedious gala.

It was just the two of them.

Scarlett was asking him if he'd like to make love with her again? Was the earth spinning?

"Hell yes!" he growled. A moment later, he was coming around to her side of the table and leaning over her as his arms wrapped around her slender figure, lifting her up so that she was completely pressed against his harder one. His mouth covered hers and he kissed her, demanding that she open her mouth, demanding entry to the sweetness that was her lips.

This wasn't the gentle loving she'd experienced the first time in this man's arms. This was a demanding, overwhelming kind of loving. And her body craved more! Scarlett wrapped her arms around his neck, her hands diving into the surprising softness of his dark hair. Her fingers were actually gripping those dark locks, afraid he might stop, afraid they would be interrupted again and she wasn't going to allow that! Not this time!

When he tore his mouth away from hers, she whimpered, but realized a split second later that it was only to move to her neck and she smiled happily as she tilted her head slightly, giving him better access and even shivering when his teeth scraped along her skin, making her body shiver with excitement.

His hands weren't still either. While hers continued to hold him close to her, worried that some silly nugget might pop into his head that would make him stop what he was doing, his hands were sliding underneath her sweater, pushing the material away so that his fingers could smooth against her skin. Good grief, she loved the way he touched her! He seemed to know exactly where all of her sensitive places were on her skin. Or maybe he just realized they were sensitive because she made some sort of sound whenever his fingers moved over that spot. She didn't care! All she cared about was begging him to do it again.

"Don't stop," she whimpered when he pulled back slightly. "Oh, please don't stop!"

Grayson shook his head. "No way!" he replied and lifted her into his arms. "But we're not doing this here," he told her and lifted her into his arms.

With her legs around his waist and his hands supporting her bottom, he carried her out of the dining room. Scarlett wasn't too interested or concerned about where he made love to her. All she cared about was having it happen, needing it to happen. So when he made it to the stairs, she was already nibbling at his neck, loving the way he smelled right there under his jaw. She felt the wall against her back and shifted her body to enjoy that hardness pressing against her core, shivering when she moved exactly right. And since it felt so good, she did it again. And again.

"Why are we stopping?" she breathed out, closing her eyes when his fingers found her nipples through the thin, lace material of her bra.

Grayson was pressing her up against the wall, his legs unable to carry her up the stairs when she pressed her heat against him like that. It felt too damn good!

"Because I can't carry you when you make those sounds, love," he told her with a deep, husky chuckle.

"I'll stop," she gasped, worried that she was doing something wrong.

He laughed again. "Don't you dare stop!" he growled right back at her. "I love it!"

Scarlett's smile lit up the foyer and she shifted once more, almost laughing when she groaned but she couldn't laugh. Not when she felt like this. She'd laugh later, she promised herself. Much later.

"Please, take off my sweater!" she cried out when his fingers slipped over her nipple once more, driving her crazy with need. "I want…" she started to say something, but she was too embarrassed by what she wanted him to do.

"Tell me," he coaxed, his fingers tweaking her nipple and causing her hips to move, yeah, just like that. "Tell me what you like, Scarlett. I love hearing words like that from you."

She opened her eyes and looked up into his darker ones. Was he serious? She bit her lip, trying to control the way her hips wanted to move against him. But she couldn't! She wanted him too badly and it was as if her body was controlled by this need instead of common sense and ladylike behavior.

Grayson obviously understood the controversy happening inside her head and chuckled. "Tell me Scarlett. Leave the lady in the living room. Give me the woman in the bedroom." And he shifted his hips ever so slightly, causing the friction he knew she liked. When she gasped and arched her body against his, he almost roared with the need that was driving him crazy. He wanted to bury himself in her heat, flood her with a need that was just as strong as what was driving him.

"Tell me," he coaxed again, leaning down and nibbling at her neck. At the same time, his fingers pulled the lace material away, his hands sliding against her very soft, very pointed nipple. "I'll do anything you want me to do, but you have to tell me."

She couldn't hold back any longer. Not when he was doing those things to her body. She needed more! So much more!

"Take off my sweater!" she commanded. "Do it now!" she told him, her eyes lighting up with the need she was feeling and unable to fight him any longer. "Please, Grayson!"

A moment later, her sweater was on the floor and he was lifting her up again as he carried her up the stairs. He almost stumbled when her pretty, white teeth took his ear lobe between them but he made it a few more steps. A moment later, he pressed her against the wall again, his deft fingers releasing the catch on her bra and tossing it behind him. He didn't care where it landed, as long as the material wasn't covering her soft, pretty breasts. He took only a moment to look down at her breasts, his mind fizzling as he noticed her beautiful, pink nipples. Just one taste, he told himself. One taste and he would….

His arms lifted her higher, high enough so that his mouth could latch onto her nipple and he sucked hard on the sensitive flesh, hard enough so that she was screaming, her legs tightening around him and his need soared impossibly higher. Just one more taste, he told himself and moved his mouth to the other breast.

Scarlett couldn't believe what her body was feeling. It was like her skin was on fire but that wasn't exactly true either because the heat was coming from inside out to her skin.

"Grayson, please!" she begged, shifting against him but he'd lifted her higher and she couldn't find that hardness any longer. And she needed it. Now!

"Please what?" he asked as he slowly lowered her back down. She wiggled her body until it was right where she wanted to be and he had to close his eyes to control the need to rip her leggings off and bury himself inside of her now.

Scarlett wasn't messing around any longer. She moved her hands from his massive shoulders to the sides of his face. Looking into his eyes, she gritted her teeth as she said, "Get us to a bedroom now, Grayson, or make love to me right here!"

Grayson heard the command and almost laughed. Normally, he would be in charge but if this little woman wanted to give some orders, he was more than happy to comply. "Your wish," he started to say but she slid her hands down from his face to his shoulders, those dainty little hands fluttering against his skin and he lost his ability to speak. He lifted her up and carried her the rest of the way to the bedroom he'd been not-sleeping in.

Laying her down on the bed, he stood up, ignoring her whimper as he pulled her leggings down her slender legs. His fingers weren't playing around this time and he pulled her underwear right along with the stretchy pants. When he looked down at her, seeing her naked, a sight he'd never thought to behold again, he had to stop and savor the moment. She was so exquisitely perfect. It was almost as if this woman was made specifically for him and he couldn't believe his luck in having her in his arms again.

He wasn't going to question that luck though. Nor was he going to stop and let her think about what was going to happen. He wanted her too badly to let his conscience start to tell him not to touch her, not to make love to her. For this moment, for this period in time, Scarlett was his. He had no idea what he'd done, what amazingly good deed he'd accomplished to warrant her in his arms, but he was going to enjoy every moment until she came to her senses. He'd apologize then. He'd beg her forgiveness and tell her that they could still be friends and he'd never hurt her again.

But until that moment, he was going to love her so thoroughly that, hopefully, he could delay the moment when she started to regret giving herself to him.

With that in mind, he bent lower and kissed her toes, working his way up her leg. He almost laughed when he discovered that the backs of her knees were ticklish but kept on moving higher and higher.

"I know what your intent is," she told him through gritted teeth. "And it isn't necessary, Grayson. Just…"

71

His mouth nibbled the soft skin on the inside of her thigh. "Shut up, Scarlett. And let me do what I want to do. You're not in charge any longer. Your time is over. It is my time now." And with that, before she could argue with him again, he moved his mouth to that part of her that he'd been working towards, that heat that tempted him beyond reason.

When her hips lifted off of the bed, he grabbed hold but wouldn't relent. Adding his fingers, sliding one inside of her heat, drove her need higher and he sucked and nibbled, creating such a point of intense sensation that, within only moments, she was splintering apart.

He smiled as he watched her climax, reveled in how responsive her body was and, as she slowly came back to him, he moved up her slender body. Looking down at her, he banked his own need. "I'm going to do that to you so often that maybe it will start to take longer before you climax and I can have a longer taste of your sweet body," he told her.

Scarlett blushed, her hand lifting to cover his mouth. "No," she told him.

His only response was to take her hand away and kiss her, denying her ability to tell him that he wasn't going to do that to her again. He loved the way she tasted and she wasn't going to get away with stopping him. Never!

When he lifted his mouth again, she was sighing with happiness but he almost laughed when she looked as if she was finished. "Oh, we're not finished, love. Not by a long shot!"

"I hope so," she smiled. But her eyes moved down his body. "Are you going to do something about those clothes?" she teased.

He smiled back at her even as his hand reached behind his head and pulled the material, tossing it behind him. When his hands moved to the snap of his jeans, she shook her head, sitting up. "Will you let me?" she asked.

He looked down at her and felt like he was going to explode. But the idea of her slender fingers touching him there was just too much of a need now that she'd offered. "Of course," he said. Or growled or grunted. He wasn't sure if he was able to speak right now.

Her fingers shook slightly as they unsnapped his jeans. The zipper was easier and he actually considered wearing clothes with only Velcro on them in the future, just so that this process would be easier and faster for her.

He waited in a moment of pleasurable agony as her fingers slid the zipper down, her fingers so shockingly close but not close enough. He wanted her fingers around him, touching him!

When she pulled the denim away, he groaned and her fingers whipped back. He could have laughed, but he was in too much pain, needing her touch. As gently as possible, he took her hands and pulled them back to him. "It's okay, love. You didn't hurt me. Just the opposite, actually." He pushed his jeans and boxers down, tossing them to the side, then guided her hand back to him, wrapping her fingers around his erection, showing her how he wanted her to hold him. And it felt better than he'd thought possible.

"No more," he groaned.

Scarlett couldn't believe that he was stopping her. She'd wanted to do that to him so badly but he was pulling her hand away and pushing her back against the mattress while he rolled a condom down his length. "But…"

"Later!" he told her and pressed her legs wider. His mouth latched onto her nipple one more time and, sure enough, she made those sexy sounds that incited his lust even higher. Moving to the other nipple, he gave that one the same attention, all the while, he was moving between her legs and pressing himself into her heat. He had to release her nipple but he grabbed her hands, lifting her arms up so that she was holding onto him as he filled up her heat. Watching her eyes, he loved the way she felt as her body clenched around his. It was so amazingly hot to watch her mouth open and feel her hips shift to adjust to his invasion. He thought he could happily die right at this moment.

But then she moved against him, her hips lifting ever so slightly and he knew that he didn't want to die. Not just yet. He needed to…yes! "Just like that, love," he told her. "Do that again."

Scarlett complied and he loved the way she shifted, the heat and gentleness of her. He wished he could repay in kind, but he was over the top with the need to feel her climax again, to find his own release.

Grabbing her hands, he lifted them up over her head so that she couldn't touch him any longer. He would lose it and he wanted her to find her own release first.

Moving as slowly as he could, he watched her eyes, trying to make this perfect for her. But in the end, he simply couldn't move slowly enough for her. She just felt too amazing. Speeding up, he tried hard not to slam into her but he suspected that he might be too rough. He was relieved when he felt her splinter apart and he wanted to help her, to make it longer but he couldn't. She just felt too good as his own climax burst over him and all he could do was hold onto her.

A long time later, he lifted himself up and rolled to the side, pulling her with him. "Sorry for crushing you," he mumbled, still breathing heavily after that explosion. Impossibly, that time was even better than the last. And he'd thought that last time couldn't get any better.

"Don't apologize," she said and snuggled closer to him, wanting to feel his skin against hers. "I loved it."

He looked down at her, one eyebrow going higher. "You liked being crushed by my weight?"

She laughed, feeling giddy. "I loved feeling your weight on me." Her hand fluttered down over his stomach and Grayson's heart almost stopped. "Too soon, love."

She pulled her hand away. "Oh. I read about that somewhere," she told him, her smile disappearing.

Grayson watched the blush form on her pretty cheeks. Rolling back, he looked down at her. "What exactly did you read?" he demanded, curious about her blush.

She let her leg slid up the outside of his hips, loving the differences in their bodies. "I read that it takes men a bit longer to..." she shrugged slightly. "Well, you know..." she cringed. "Do it again."

Grayson was so stunned by what she was implying that it took him a moment to react. When he finally did, he could only throw back his head and laugh. "Oh really? So you think..." his eyes moved down her nakedness, unable to hold back another chuckle. "You think that I can only do it once."

She shook her head. "Oh no. I know that you can do it twice. Remember the last time?"

He did. And his eyes turned serious. He opened his mouth, about to apologize but she slapped her hand over his mouth.

Scarlett shook her head. "No Grayson. Don't you dare say a word. Nothing that will change how happy I feel right now. The only words you can utter are instructions on how long it will take before we can enjoy that activity once again." She carefully lifted her hand away from his mouth, fully aware that he could have easily pinned her arms against the mattress and said anything he wanted. He was too strong and could easily overcome her pathetic attempts to stop him, but she was grateful that he'd allowed her to speak.

"I think," he told her as his hand moved along her waist, cupping her breast one more time, "that I need to prove that the article you read was completely wrong." His eyes watched her nipple pucker as his thumb traced the delicate skin. "Or at least when you're in my arms." And he proceeded to do just that. Thoroughly!

Chapter 10

Over the next two weeks, Scarlett was happier than she'd ever thought possible. She woke up every morning in Grayson's arms. They worked in the castle together, but he respected her need for space while dealing with the contractors renovating the various rooms, and she tried to keep the noise to a minimum so that he could concentrate on his work.

She met him for lunch every day though. Sometimes he would find her with a picnic basket and take her out to one of the meadows, spread out a big blanket and they would share the meal under the warm sunshine. Other times, when it was rainy or just a dull, dreary day, they would eat in the kitchen which she'd transformed into a bright, happy place to be.

But the evenings…! Goodness, the evenings were the best! Every night, they dined by candlelight, discussing the progress they'd made throughout the day, sipping wine and eating whatever delicious meal his assistant had procured for them. Somehow, the amazing woman was able to find unique meals that were delivered hot to the door, complete with a decadent dessert.

Scarlett would be gaining weight with all of the rich food she was eating but Grayson's efforts kept her waistline in check. Because of the nights! After dinner, he would take her into his arms and make love to her until both of them were too weak to move. Only at that point, would they fall asleep in each other's arms. Normally, he would wake her up at some point in the night and make love to her again. Or sometimes, he would hold her gently in his arms, keeping her warm and feeling secure. Until the morning when he would make love to her once more. In the shower, against the bedroom wall, the hallway…sometimes actually in the bed! It was the most erotic time in her life.

And she never wanted it to end.

Chapter 11

"Hey," Grayson whispered softly, trying to wake up a sleepy Scarlett.

Scarlett rolled over and opened her eyes slightly. When she saw his handsome face, she smiled despite her exhaustion. "Good morning," she whispered, lifting her hands to touch his cheek.

"I have to go somewhere over the next few days but I'm leaving a team of bodyguards here to make sure you are safe," he told her. "Will you be okay?"

Huh? Scarlett stared up at him for a long moment, trying to force her mind to understand what he was telling her. When it finally sunk in, that he was leaving her, that he was going away, the message broke through her exhaustion more quickly and she tried to sit up. "What do you mean? Why do you have to leave?" She also realized that he was not only showered, but fully dressed in a suit and tie. He hadn't worn a suit since the day he'd arrived. They'd maintained a casual existence here in the Scottish countryside, wearing jeans and sweaters or sweatshirts. She swallowed the panic as she held the sheet over her nakedness.

"I have to but it will only be for a few days if I can get things done quickly," he told her firmly. "Will you be okay?"

Scarlett thought about it for a long moment. No, she wasn't going to be okay. He was leaving her! They'd had such an incredible few weeks together and now he was just leaving her? How could he do that? Hadn't this time together been as special to him as it had been for her?

She wasn't sure what he was telling her, but she'd always known that this time would come. Grayson was not the forever kind of man. He was the love 'em and leave 'em kind. She'd known that since she was a teenager and she'd known it from the moment she'd fallen in love with him. All she'd wanted at the beginning of this affair was a few more nights in his arms and she'd had more than that over the past two weeks. So it was time for her to release her hopes and dreams and accept that this was over between them.

Swallowing hard, she banked all of her pain over his departure behind a weak smile. "Yes. I'll be fine," she lied.

He kissed her forehead and walked away, leaving her gaping after him.

"He left?" she said to the now-empty bedroom. "Why?" She felt so lost, so desolate now. It was over. She'd experienced glorious nights in his arms. But they hadn't been as special to him as they had been to her. Obviously.

Why though? How could he not have felt the amazing passion that flared up whenever they were close to each other? And it hadn't diminished, not at all over the past two weeks. In fact, it had only intensified. So why was he leaving?

But the empty doorway didn't have any answers for her. All she saw was the dark, lonely hallway without any Grayson coming through the door to hand her a cup of coffee. Good grief, they'd even gotten a second coffee machine just so both of them could make their own coffee and not have to endure the other person's! Everything had been so wonderful! What had gone wrong? Why had he had to leave?

She flopped back onto the bed and stared up at the ceiling. How many times had she done this in the past, wondering about that man?

She wanted to yell and scream at him, she was so furious. He couldn't do this to her again! But he had! He'd just left her! He'd left everything that they'd shared over the past two weeks and just dumped her cold. She was no different from all the other women who had shared his bed and his amazing body over the years. She hadn't even lasted as long as some of them!

She flung the covers off of her and stomped furiously to the bathroom. "No more!" As she scrubbed her body clean, trying to forget how many times they'd showered together in this bathroom, she swore to herself that she was going to get over that man! She would fall in love with someone else. She would find another man who could make her feel this alive. This wonderful!

She wasn't aware of the tears on her cheeks because the shower kept rinsing them off. She was brutally aware of the pain in her heart at his rejection, the humiliation that she couldn't hold his interest longer than some of the other women in his past and the fury that he was just too obtuse to know how wonderful they were together.

Over the next week, she went into overdrive. She was determined to finish this project off and get out of the castle. Every time she moved into a different room, something hit her hard about her time here with Grayson. They'd made love in practically every room, every piece of furniture and it hurt to remember how incredible his touch had felt, knowing that she'd never feel it again. She couldn't handle it. This hurt way too much.

So she worked like a maniac, getting in additional contractors, making the castle into an amazing showpiece, but she used a lot of her own money to pay for the overtime of the workers. And she added special details that she normally wouldn't, simply because this was Harrison and Sierra's "hideaway". She brought in special doors, prettier lights, anything that would make this wonderful castle into a home.

And every time she came up with a new idea, she prayed that Sierra and Harrison would find more happiness here than she had with Grayson.

Oh, that wasn't completely true. She wasn't sure that they could be nearly as happy as she'd been. Scarlett admitted that her time with Grayson had been more joyful than she could have ever thought possible. He was a sweet, gentle yet demanding lover and he taught her things she'd never thought her body could do, could achieve.

Whenever she found herself in a room where the memories were too overwhelming, she'd hurry out and go for a run, letting the fresh, moist air clear her mind. And because they had been in all of those rooms so often and there were so many memories, she got a lot of miles in during the last few days.

In record time, she was finished. The six bedrooms looked wonderful, both elegant and comfortable. She was proud of the way they all looked like showpieces but still invited a person to curl up onto the bed or a cozy chair to read.

The bathrooms were updated, the kitchen finished…the whole house was a masterpiece with new windows, fresh paint and beautiful furniture that invited a person to come into each room and sit for a spell. She could honestly say that, this castle with all of the extra little details she'd added into the effort, was her best work ever.

Unfortunately, she was a mess! After trying to sleep upstairs in the bed she'd shared with Grayson, Scarlett accepted that it simply wasn't going to happen. It was hard enough working in the various rooms, she couldn't sleep in a bed where Grayson had held her in his arms.

She'd finally broken down and moved into the local inn, unable to sleep in the castle overnight because Grayson was no longer there with her. And all of the memories of their time together, their nights and the laughter during the days, were a memory that she would cherish, but she couldn't keep thinking of it right now.

Maybe in time, she thought. Maybe she would get through the pain of his rejection and the short time they'd had together and smile at her brief love affair with the man of her dreams. But right now, all she wanted to do was to curl up into a ball and cry out her sorrow that she didn't get to hold him any longer.

Scarlett had no idea what she was going to do when their group got together for their dinners or lunches. In the past, those gatherings had been happy times, filled with teasing and laughter, not to mention just the unspoken support that each member of the group knew was there.

She knew that she couldn't face Grayson. Not right now. The memories were too sharp, too new. Even as she wandered through the rooms of the castle on her final check to make sure everything was ready for Sierra and Harrison, it felt like she could still smell Grayson in each of the rooms, his aftershave and just his manly scent. It was nice, but also very painful.

With a deep sigh and a resolution that she was not going to cry about the end of her dream affair any longer, Scarlett closed the door for the final time, ensuring that it was firmly locked, and then walked away. The SUV filled with the remaining bodyguards Grayson had left behind was waiting to take her to the airport. Unfortunately, she had no idea where she was going. She should have made reservations but she hadn't been able to dial the number, her mind unable to move beyond this castle, this project. This dream.

She knew she had other clients waiting. So it made sense that she should go back to New York and check in with her team, find out what was up next or if any other clients had called to ask for assistance, but she couldn't do it.

As the vehicle pulled away, the tears streamed down her cheeks. She couldn't believe that Grayson had walked away from what they'd had together. Was there another woman?

A sudden thought occurred to her, lifting her spirits slightly. Maybe it had only been a business crisis that needed his presence. Didn't an empire as large as his have problems that only he could deal with most of the time? It made sense, but then her hope crashed as reality set in. Grayson didn't have crises, she told herself. He was smart enough to anticipate issues and circumvent them. Not only that, he had built up his business on good sense and strong employees. His management team could handle just about anything.

But still...She glanced at her phone, praying to find some message from Grayson explaining what had happened or where he was. Or even better, that he was coming back to her.

But the phone was blank except for work issues and her shoulders slumped while her back once again rested against the smooth leather of the passenger seat. No message from Grayson. No explanation or brief text letting her know that she would see him soon. Nothing.

The business issues she skipped through were ignored because her mind simply couldn't deal with them at this point. She'd deal with those, but not today, she told herself. Tomorrow, she thought. She'd deal with that tomorrow. She smiled at that. She was channeling her inner O'Hara with those words, but then she realized that her "Rhett" wasn't trying to trick her into marriage like in the movie.

Instead of heading back to New York, for the first time in her career, she didn't check in with her assistant, nor did she call any of the clients who had sent her messages. She told Grayson's team of bodyguards that she was going to London and wouldn't need them any longer.

"But..." the captain of the team started to say, wanting to argue with her.

Scarlett shook her head and lifted her hand into the air. "No. I'm taking the train to London so, thank you for your diligence, but I'll be fine on my own now." With that, she stepped out of the vehicle and walked into the train station, rolling her bags behind her. She bought a ticket to London, found a seat on the train and then stared out the window the entire trip. She didn't see the beautiful countryside. In fact, she refused to let herself think at all. She didn't want to think because thinking caused her to wonder about what she'd done wrong with Grayson. And that hurt. She was tired of hurting. She was tired of wondering and dreaming and hoping and feeling the debilitating disappointment when her hopes and dreams weren't going to come true.

When she reached London, she considered making her way to Harrison's building, maybe even calling up Sierra and asking if she could stay overnight, just until she figured out what she could do. But in the end, she simply checked into a hotel room, wanting to be alone so that she could try to heal. And figure out how she was going to get over the most amazing man she'd ever met.

Chapter 12

"Oh man, have you messed up," Damon said as he stood in the doorway, looking at Grayson's furious expression.

Grayson ignored the man, pushing into the house. "Is she here?" he demanded. He was tired, sick of traveling since he'd been to three different countries in one week, disgusted with his "friends", every one of whom had relayed various forms of "Finally!" when he'd presented his side of the issue to them, not to mention he was frustrated that Scarlett wasn't where he'd left her and in no mood to deal with Damon's humor right now.

Harrison stepped into the villa's foyer, leaning a muscular shoulder against the doorframe. "She's here, but she doesn't want to see you."

Grayson's eyes narrowed as he saw the man he'd just left a few days ago stepping into the room. Why the hell was Harrison here? Why wasn't he in London? Wait a minute, he thought, Harrison mentioned he had something in Paris he was dealing with. Why the hell was he here, looking smug and...angry?

Further compounding the issue, Malik stepped into the area, followed by Stefan as well, all four men glaring at Grayson furiously. The tension in the room was vaguely reminiscent of the old days, right before one of them was going to start a fight. And oddly enough, Grayson was just frustrated enough to take them all on. At least if he was fighting, he wouldn't have to deal with the worry, the panic he was feeling as he tried to hunt down the one woman who should be sitting in a castle in Scotland. But she wasn't! He'd just about fired his entire security staff when he found out that Scarlett wasn't with them. In the end, he knew that it was his fault that they'd let her leave. He'd only instructed them on the dangers she was facing at the castle. He hadn't yet informed them that Scarlett was going to be their permanent assignment.

"What the hell is going on?" Grayson demanded, taking that fighting stance that had gotten them into so much trouble in school.

Stefan shook his head, recognizing the heat in his friend's eyes but unwilling to give Grayson what he was obviously shooting for. "You messed up."

"Bad," Harrison agreed, shaking his head as if he were ashamed somehow.

Malik was much more direct. He wasn't going to let any ambiguity enter into this fight. He was ready to pound Grayson to a pulp for the pain he'd caused but wanted the man to know why he was about to be pulverized. "I thought you were going to propose to her!" Malik stated as if Grayson was the biggest idiot in the world.

Finally! Someone was making sense! Well, a little sense, he thought. "I am!" Grayson yelled back, throwing his hands up in the air. "Just as soon as I can find the woman, I'll put the damn ring on her finger! So if she's here, you had all better get out of my way. Because I'm tired and I want that woman in front of me right now!"

"You don't deserve her!" This came from Sasha who had stepped into the middle of the tall men. She looked like a furious kitten in the midst of all of the lions surrounding her. "You hurt her! She trusted you and you just walked away from her without any explanation!"

Grayson stared down at the dark haired woman with confused eyes. "I went to get..."

Sierra's sandy blond head poked around her husband and came to stand next to Sasha. "You left her! It doesn't matter where you went, you didn't tell her where you were going and she's now hurt. She's decided to fall in love with someone else."

Those were fighting words! "Like hell she is!" Grayson roared. "Scarlett! Get out here. Now!" He knew that he couldn't get around these ladies, especially when Livia and Jina joined their pretty ranks.

"No!" he heard Scarlett yell back.

Grayson looked at all of the men surrounding him. Gone was the anger and he was now even more perplexed because each had an amused expression on their faces. Grayson understood that they'd all gone through this with their women but, in his mind, that should mean the men should be helping him, not standing by their women when his own woman was hiding from him. "Why aren't you helping me?" he demanded of his longtime friends.

The men either threw back their heads, laughing, or they punched him on the arm. "Welcome to the club, my man. You're in what we call 'the pit of anger' and it is damn hard to climb out of." Malik explained.

He looked at each of them, stunned and furious. "And you're not going to help in any way?" Grayson asked, glaring at the man.

Malik lifted his hands up in the air as if he were about to be arrested. "And get my woman mad at me? Hell no," he told Grayson and stepped back.

Grayson looked at each of the other men, all of whom were nodding their heads, looking at their lovely wives in turn and then back at Grayson. Their silent message was clear; "I'm not messing up my good thing to help you. You're on your own."

Grayson could not believe that his friends were abandoning him to the tender mercies of their wives. And there was nothing he could do about it. He couldn't go through them because he might hurt them. And he liked them too much to do that.

But his woman was hiding from him and that he would not allow. "Scarlett, I'm sorry, love. I didn't mean to hurt you," he called out, trying to figure out what words he could give her to make this all right. He wasn't even sure what was wrong, he just knew that she'd thought he'd left her. In reality, he'd dragged his pilot and flight crew all over the world, trying to reach each of these men and explain that he and Scarlett were in love and he was going to marry her. It was his way of asking for her hand in marriage, but Scarlett didn't have a father. Hell, she didn't even have an uncle any longer. What she did have were four very large, very annoying "brothers" who were more than willing to make his life hell for a while.

He saw her then and his heart twisted at the sight in front of her. He almost punched Malik when the man put his arm around Scarlett's shoulders, offering his woman comfort when it should be his shoulder she was crying on. But he focused only on her red-rimmed eyes, her red, button nose and the tears that were still evident in her beautiful eyes.

"You finally loved me," she said, her chin quivering. "You finally came to me and everything seemed so perfect. We were friends and then…" she didn't say the words but glanced up at the four other men warily. They all looked at her, then at Grayson. Each of them took a step forward, more than ready to pound him because they understood that Grayson had "been" with Scarlett. Luckily, the ladies came to his rescue. They instantly knew what was going to happen and turned around, glaring their husbands into halting. "Don't you dare!" Jina said for all of the ladies. "Unless you want to be hypocrites, then just back off and let him say what he needs to say."

The men stopped, but they didn't like it. They still glared at Grayson, furious big brothers, ready to defend their "sister's" honor.

In that moment, he knew he was going to send an enormous bouquet of flowers to each lovely lady for sticking up for him. For the moment, though, he focused all of his attention on the one woman he needed by his side. "I love you, Scarlett," he said, frustrated because this was something he had planned to say in private. Declaring his feelings for this woman in front of an audience was damn awkward. But he'd do it if that was what it took to get her by his side. "I love you and there isn't another woman who has ever compared to you. You've driven me crazy since you turned into a teenager and you've only become more beautiful over the years. I've loved you this whole time."

Her jaw dropped. "But all those other women!"

He shook his head. "They were nothing," he told her. "I loved you!"

"But…" she lifted her hands, narrowing her eyes at his words. "Don't you dare try to tell me that you didn't have sex with them!"

He clenched his teeth. "No. I can't claim that. But I didn't know that you loved me as well, Scarlett. I had no idea that there was even a chance that you might feel the same way towards me, love. You have to admit, we've been close friends for years."

She conceded that point only with a slight shrug of her dainty shoulder. "Why did you leave Scotland?" she demanded, swiping an errant tear that slipped off of her lashes. "Everything felt so perfect and then you just left. You said goodbye as if that was the end."

Grayson couldn't believe she'd so completely misinterpreted his actions. "I didn't, honey! Or if I sounded that way, that's definitely not what I meant to convey," he claimed furiously! Then he thought back, trying to remember the words. "Oh hell!" he grumbled. Looking around at the others, he glared at the men who were still "protecting" Scarlett from him. "Would any of you like to explain to her what I have been doing for the past several days?"

All four men simply shrugged their shoulders, keeping silent. "This is your party," Harrison finally said.

When the others remained silent, he glared at them. "Really?" he snapped back at them.

Jina, Sasha, Livia and Sierra all turned around again, crossing their arms over their chests. "Boys, do you have something you need to tell us?"

The men just shook their heads, trying to look innocent. But it wasn't working. The ladies turned around and looked at Grayson, their expressions not so angry now. "Go ahead. What have you been doing?"

Grayson's hands were fisted on his hips. "I've been flying to their places, making sure they were okay with me proposing to Scarlett! I was respecting their friendship with my woman!"

The ladies turned back to face their husbands, Jina's mouth hanging open as she stared up at her handsome husband with rising anger. "Why didn't you tell Scarlett this when she came in here crying earlier today?"

When the men all shrugged their shoulders again, Grayson decided turnabout was fair play. "Because they all had to flounder to get you ladies back," Grayson explained, a smug smile forming on his features as the truth hit the ladies. "And they wanted me to have to climb out of the pit as well!"

Harrison chuckled, only confirming Grayson's words. "Entertainment value, my man!"

Sierra instantly whipped around, her eyes narrowing on her husband. "You knew about this? And you didn't say anything? Even when Scarlett was sobbing away, obviously in pain and you knew what was happening?"

"Of course he knew! Everyone of them knew," Grayson announced and waited patiently as their wives absorbed the news. He kept glancing back to Scarlett though. Sending his friends into trouble with their wives was fine but this was all about Scarlett and trying to get his ring on her finger. Forever!

The wives each looked at their husbands, all of whom instantly knew that they were now in trouble. "It was amusing," Malik said to Jina as an explanation for his omission. Jina jabbed his stomach with her elbow for that and Malik grunted as if he were in pain, just to humor his lovely wife. They all knew that she hadn't even bruised him slightly. Nor had she genuinely tried to hurt him. Jina might be angry with him, but she wouldn't do anything that might physically or emotionally hurt the man she loved to distraction.

Sasha punched her husband's rock hard shoulder but only got another chuckle. Damon then wrapped his hand around her now-sore knuckles. "Sorry, love. It was just too hilarious an opportunity to pass up." At his wife's narrowed eyes he continued. "Come on, they've been madly in love with each other for years! Even you ladies instantly knew it as soon as each of you saw the two of them together!" He was looking down at his still-angry wife. "Admit it, there was a bit of humor in this whole situation."

"No!" Sasha told him. "It definitely wasn't funny! I've been in Scarlett's shoes and I know how painful it is to..." she stopped, remembering what it was like when she'd thought that Damon was in love with Scarlett. She bowed her head, pretending to be truly upset. Oh, she was good and mad! But she also knew her husband and there was no way he would allow Scarlett to be hurt for too long. Eventually, one of these men would have clued her in on what was going on.

But of course, Damon was instantly worried that he'd hurt his wife and moved closer. "Sasha," he said, floundering to figure out how to make things better. "I'm sorry, love..."

And that was all she needed. Lifting her head, she glared at her husband. "Apologize to Scarlett!" she snapped, "Maybe then I'll forgive you."

In typical brotherly fashion, the men looked over at Scarlett who was furious that they would pull this kind of trick on her. "You all knew about this?" she demanded, looking at each one in turn. And then she whipped around, glaring at Grayson. "And you went to them," she said scathingly, "to see if it was *okay* if we got married?!" With each word, she stepped closer to Grayson, her shoulders tense and her hands fisted at her sides. "Why didn't you ask *me* if it was okay to marry *me*?! Or are all of those men going to be in our marriage bed with us?"

The men all chuckled, relieved once again that it was their friend in the hot seat once again. Grayson knew he was in more trouble now. "Wait a minute, Scarlett," he said, lifting his hands to placate her. "I think you're twisting things around slightly. I only…" he looked around, pleading for help but the men were still looking amused and the ladies were…well, they were looking hopeful.

He turned back to face Scarlett, trying desperately to find the words to reassure her. After all these years of loving her, he still couldn't believe that she could feel the same way. She was just so beautiful and so amazing…

"Here's the thing, Scarlett," he muttered, moving closer to her, trying to put an arm around her shoulder but she pushed it off. With a sigh, he took her hand. "Scarlett, you know how the six of us have been over the years! Those guys, they're like your big brothers and you damn well know it! And since," he paused, his voice lowering, "since Uncle Charles died, I didn't have anyone to ask. I was…"

Scarlett instantly understood and all of her anger dissipated. "You were asking those horrible men for my hand in marriage. Right?" trying to encourage him, to fill in the awkward silence when he struggled to explain.

"Yes," he replied gently, relieved that she finally understood what he had been attempting to do.

Scarlett moved closer, her hands cupping his jaw tenderly and with all the love she was feeling. "Grayson, you needed to ask me. You should have known that those idiots would do something horrible to you. It's just their way." She heard a few grunts of disagreement but she ignored them. Especially when she heard the ladies of the group shush each man in turn. No one wanted to hear their protestations of innocence at this point.

And she slipped into his arms, wrapping her own around his lean waist and laying her cheek against his chest.

"Wait a minute," Stefan straightened from his indolent position against the wall. "You can't forgive him that easily!"

Malik agreed. "He walked out on you, honey. You need to…" He stopped when Jina jabbed him in the stomach again. He instantly grabbed her, pulling her closer so she couldn't try again. "He should…"

"Grovel!" Damon asserted moments before Sasha's hand covered his mouth.

"He should…" Harrison tried to add his advice, but Sierra's glare told him he should just shut up. He chuckled and pulled his wife against his side. "By the way, old man, the castle is a wedding gift." Sierra's smile brightened with excitement and Harrison squeezed her gently, demonstrating his love and silently telling her that she'd had a good idea.

The ladies quickly herded their obnoxious husbands out of the foyer, giving Grayson and Scarlett some privacy.

When they were finally alone, Grayson looked down at the woman he loved so painfully, he could barely breathe sometimes.

He pulled a ring out of his pocket, the ring that he'd bought weeks ago. "I've been carrying this around for way too long. I was hoping to find a better place to ask you," he said and took her hand, "but under the circumstances, I'm not going to wait any longer." Looking into her pretty, blue eyes, he said, "Scarlett, please marry me. If I'd known that you loved me the way I loved you, I would have proposed years ago. But I promise I won't be a fool again. I'll…"

"Yes!" she cried and lifted up on her toes while, at the same time, pulling his head down so that she could kiss him. "Yes!" she muttered in between breathtaking kisses.

Epilogue

Scarlett stood at the back of the church, her mind spinning with excitement and hope.

"You okay?" Sasha asked, seeing the look in Scarlett's eyes and not sure what to make of it.

Scarlett turned and noticed four sets of eyes that were looking at her as if she might faint. "Everything is perfect," she replied, afraid to move for fear that this was a dream and she might wake up.

The music changed and the ladies all took their places. "Well, if you're sure you want to go through with this," Sierra commented, as if to say Scarlett was crazy to enter into a marriage with Grayson.

Scarlett laughed. "Like you would let another woman marry your man?" she suggested.

Sierra chuckled. "Not a chance," she replied.

"I thought so," she said. Sierra was almost as much in love with Harrison as Scarlett was with Grayson.

"You look beautiful," Jina said, giving Scarlett a gentle hug.

Scarlett sighed happily. "Thank you." Her eyes once again moved to the double doors, worry coming back into their blue depths. "Is he really…?"

Sasha stepped closer. "He's not only there, waiting for you at the front of the church, but he's been asking the same question to the guys for the past two hours."

Livia nodded her head. "If you don't marry the man soon, he's going to just pick you up and carry you off."

Scarlett definitely wouldn't mind that. Not one little bit!

But the sound of the music increased just as the wedding coordinator opened the double doors. One by one, the ladies stepped forward and walked down the aisle.

Finally, it was her moment. She straightened her dress and moved into place. Just as the music changed, she took a deep breath, clenched the stems of her flowers and looked up, right into the eyes of her man.

After a month of crazy meetings, fittings, making decisions about flowers, food, the cake and location, she was finally hiere, finally about to marry Grayson.

Grayson couldn't believe how beautiful Scarlett looked. It was almost as if he could see her blue eyes even as she stared at the back of the church and his whole body puffed up with pride that this was soon to be his wife. His woman!

The past month had been furiously tedious. He didn't understand why they couldn't have just gotten married. But now, seeing her in the flowing, white dress, seeing the happiness he was feeling reflected in her eyes and Grayson knew that the wait was well worth it. He'd do just about anything for this woman.

He knew that he was going to do just about everything to her. As soon as he had her alone, he would start that exploration, he promised himself.

"You're staring," Malik teased, punching Grayson on the shoulder.

Grayson ignored him, continuing to look at his woman as she stepped closer and closer to him.

"He's supposed to be staring, you ass," Harrison commented. Vaguely, he heard Stefan and Damon comment about something but he ignored all of them. After all the pranks they'd played on him this month, he was ready to just tie them all up until he was properly wed to Scarlett. He didn't trust them, not an inch, to mess things up for him.

Damn, she was beautiful, he thought. Just a few more steps.

Moving forward, he took her hand in his and pulled her closer, wanting to feel everything about her. "You look amazing," he told her. He was rewarded for his month long wait by the smile in her eyes with his words. Never before had any woman made him wait. Not like his Scarlett. But it was all worth it.

The minister started the service and Grayson thought about his beginnings, the parents he never knew, the scholarship to the boarding school and all the fights he'd initiated or ended when the other students didn't accept him.

But now he was standing next to the most beautiful woman in the world and she was about to become his wife. His woman! Scarlett was his, finally! After years of loving her, he would finally have her by his side.

"Do you take…" Scarlett stopped listening. Yes. The answer was always yes! When the minister paused, she smiled up at Grayson and slid the platinum ring onto his finger. "I do," she finally said, relieved to be able to say those words.

"Do you take…" Grayson waited impatiently. But before the minister even finished, his voice rang out, "I do." He looked down at her fingers, sliding the platinum and diamond ring down her slender fingers and then closed his own around them as if to say that she could never take the ring off.

"I now pronounce you husband and wife," the minister announced.

Grayson didn't wait for permission. As soon as the words were spoken, he took Scarlett into his arms. Kissing her was better than breathing, he thought.

The music started up and he lifted his head, seeing the sparkle of tears in her eyes. "You okay?" he asked, running a finger down her soft cheek.

"Better than okay," she replied.

Grayson squeezed her fingers, thought about kissing her once again, but knew it would be better if he could get her alone. Turning around, he faced the crowd that was already on their feet, cheering loudly. There were friends and clients and people he didn't know or give a damn about. The only people he cared about were the ones by his side and behind him as they filed out of the church.

As soon as they were out in the narthex, he pulled Scarlett to the side and kissed her more thoroughly.

"You're mine now," he growled a moment before his lips covered hers.

Scarlett laughed, delighted with her handsome husband. Throwing her arms around his neck, she lifted herself up higher. "I've always been yours, my love."

Excerpt from Pregnant with the Sheik's Baby
Book 1 in The Samara Royal Family Series

Mia Fortelle stared up at the beautiful dress on display with longing, completely oblivious to the biting, cold wind or the other pedestrians rushing around her. "Goodness, wouldn't that be lovely," Mia sighed as she looked through the store's window, practically drooling over the beautiful coat made of warm, red wool. Or it might be cashmere. Mia had no idea, nor could she afford either. In fact, she couldn't afford anything more than a wistful stare through the window. That particular coat from this designer probably cost as much as a whole month's salary. Possibly even two months', she thought with grim acceptance as she pulled her boring, brown tweed coat closer around her body, trying to stave off the frigid cold of yet another brutal Montreal winter. A teacher's salary wasn't a whole lot so a month's paycheck probably wouldn't cover that coat. Maybe the scarf, she thought with a chuckle.

"You should get it," a deep voice said to her right.

Mia spun around to smile politely. She'd anticipated possibly the store manager or maybe just a passerby.

What she hadn't anticipated, never could have imagined, was looking into the eyes of the most amazing man she'd ever seen in her life. Tall, extremely tall, with black hair and dark eyes, tanned skin, a hard nose and even harder jawline that was a bit darker than the rest of his face as his end-of-day beard made its presence known.

He was shockingly attractive and her body shivered once again, but this time, it wasn't because of the cold. It was because of the man, his eyes, the way he was looking at her and the swell of feminine awareness that crept up inside of her with this man standing so close.

She opened her mouth to speak, but the words wouldn't come. She was stunned by the amazing, shocking appeal of this man and not sure how to deal with such raw masculinity.

This wasn't the kind of man she normally dealt with during her day. The most masculine man she'd come across during her weekly errands was the rough guy behind the meat counter with an enormous belly and a net over his beard.

This man was...he was...beyond words. He was compelling in a sensual, erotic way that instantly made her body throb with the need to press herself against him and find out what his mouth would feel like against her lips.

Never before had any man affected her so strongly and so instantly.

And he terrified her! She wasn't the kind of woman who could handle a man like him!

"I'm sorry," she said and bowed her head, starting to step around him so that she could hurry home. She stopped at this store every day, looking at the beautiful clothes that were changed out about every two weeks. It wasn't even that she could wear those clothes, she told herself firmly as she prepared to walk away. Those clothes, and this man, were way out of her league. She was bowling alley, onion rings and movie theatre popcorn while this man was ballrooms, caviar and the best champagne. His tan, cashmere coat looked soft and warm as did the silk-lined scarf around his neck. The freezing wind was blowing his black hair, but she could tell that even that was an expensive haircut. Everything about him screamed wealth and power – two things she didn't have, nor could she ever have with her career goals.

And that was okay! She loved her job, loved her kids and thrived on teaching. What wasn't okay was the nervous way this man made her feel even as he stood two feet away from her. She didn't like the way her knees wobbled or her heart pounded inside her chest.

"Please don't go," his deep voice urged and she felt his gloved hand reach out to gently touch the sleeve of her coat. Even through the thick layer of her winter coat as well as the sleeve of her sweater underneath, she still could feel the heat of his fingers and it was like a shock wave smashing through her senses.

Looking up into his dark eyes, she was so startled, she wasn't sure what to say.

"Have dinner with me tonight," he urged.

Mia shivered, those dark eyes promising her so much more than dinner. And a very large part of her brain wondered if she should accept. Just once in her life, she wanted to live on the wild side, to experience the kind of excitement this man's eyes promised.

She opened her mouth to accept, to tell him yes and to find out more of that promise. But instead of agreeing to dinner, she shook her head. "I can't," she finally said even though she desperately wanted to say yes, which didn't make any sense since all of her instincts were telling her to run away from this dangerous man. Why would she even hesitate? Why was she still standing here? Why was she looking up at this man as if she wanted to...do things that were so very wrong?

"Can't?" he asked with a slight uplifting of those firm lips.

Ramzi watched the woman's eyes, saw the indecision and knew that he was going to have this woman. He'd been watching her for several minutes, captured by the beautiful profile as she gazed into the window of the store. He wanted her. He couldn't tell what her body was like because of the cheap, ugly winter coat, but he suspected she would be perfect. He was determined to find out just how perfect she really was. He actually had to restrain himself from reaching out and touching her porcelain skin.

And those eyes! They looked like sparkling aquamarine gems surrounded by a thick fan of dark lashes. Everything this beautiful, entrancing woman was thinking was revealed in those shining depths. Never before had he seen such a color and he knew he could lose himself in that aquamarine gaze.

"I don't think 'can't' is in my vocabulary," he teased. He caught the slight smile on her full lips a moment before she tried to hide it but it gave him courage. She started to step backwards but he took her hand, noticed the trembling even through her leather glove. "I'm not going to hurt you and I'm sorry if I'm scaring you. That isn't my intention at all. I just would like to get to know you." He paused slightly. "Perhaps if you just gave me your name, I would be satisfied."

Mia laughed despite her nervousness. "I have a sneaking suspicion that giving you my name might only encourage you." She knew that he was teasing her but she was so out of her depth with his kind of charm. "I have to go," she said through stiff lips.

"Is your husband waiting for you?" he asked, once again stepping in her path so she had to stop.

The lovely woman immediately shook her head. "I'm not married," she replied quickly.

Something relaxed inside of him. "Boyfriend then?" he asked carefully. He wasn't willing to step into a marriage, but a boyfriend could be dismissed.

"I don't..." she started to say, then shook her head again. "I'm sorry, but I don't know you and I don't normally talk to strangers. My only excuse is that you're very charming and extremely handsome. But even so, you'll have to excuse me," she said and once again moved to step around him.

Ramzi allowed her to leave this time but he nodded to his bodyguard, indicating that the man should follow the woman with the dazzling eyes and the delightful smile. "We'll meet again," he told her, enjoying the way she peeked back towards him. And there it was, he thought with relish. A barely-there smile. Some might even say a challenging smile. That's all the encouragement he needed.

Well, he didn't even need that. He was confident enough to believe he could overcome any objections she might have to their relationship, but the smile helped. It told him so much more than just a smile. It told him that she was interested.

Ah, little lady, he thought, your days are numbered. We will be together.

By six o'clock that evening, he had a file folder with the woman's information and he sat down with a glass of scotch to read.

In his experience, women were fickle, gravitating to the man who would give them the most but ready to move on to the next if something better entered their periphery. Normally, he was the "something better" that women eyed. Too many times, he'd seen women hanging off of one man's arm only to get him in their sites and abandon their date/lover/husband.

He knew that he was cynical about the world. And there were probably women out there who weren't so mercenary. But so far, he hadn't run into one of them. Was this lovely Mia of the loyal-never-before-experienced members of the female gender?

He doubted it. He wasn't that lucky, he thought with cynicism.

She was certainly lovely enough to explore though.

She was twenty-four years old, two years out of university and working on her master's degree in education. She received excellent annual evaluations from both her supervisors as well as several letters of thanks from grateful parents of students in her class and, according to the interviews from some of the parents of her students, they all loved her. Her bank balance was painfully low, she had sadly lost both of her parents several years ago and was an only child. He absently wondered if she ever got lonely now that she was alone in the world.

Moving further into the quickly compiled report, he read through the list of her professional associations, all very impressive, plus several articles that she'd had published during her years at university as well as several more published in professional journals more recently.

The information was revealing, he thought as he set the file aside, but not nearly enough. The file didn't tell him all that he wanted to know. Soon, he thought. He'd get all of the information about his mysterious, shy lady very soon.

He didn't question why he needed details about this particular woman when in the past, his relationships had always remained much more superficial. A beautiful woman, intelligent conversation and a sensuous nature were all that he wanted or required from his female companionship. Well, and the ability to forget her when his interest waned.

He suspected that Ms. Fortelle was going to be a much more fascinating companion than his previous lovers had been.

The following day, Mia stood in her classroom doorway and stared at the enormous bouquet of pink roses sitting on her desk. She didn't want to touch them but kept telling herself that they weren't poisonous, that a snake wasn't going to jump out to bite her and there was no spider lurking within the beautiful blooms, ready to attack.

They were just flowers. Simple, beautiful flowers. Pink roses. No cliché red roses from that man.

Of course, the flowers might have been from someone else, she thought. They could be from that guy she'd met at the coffee shop last week, the one with the weird dimple in the middle of one cheek but not the other. They could be from that professor she'd spoken to at the teaching conference last month, the one where everyone had been bored out of their minds. He'd been a very handsome man, if slightly more lean than the man who had occupied her thoughts and her dreams for the past twenty hours.

"Are we going into the classroom, Ms. Fortelle?" one of her students asked.

Mia looked behind her, realized that her class was still standing outside in the hallway. She'd just walked all of them back from their music class and was trying to mentally prepare for their afternoon math session when she'd spotted the flowers that had been placed on the corner of her desk.

"Oooh! Ms. Fortelle got flowers!" one of the girls exclaimed, rushing past Mia and wiggling between the desks until she was standing at the corner of Mia's desk where the roses were perched. With that announcement, chaos erupted with all of the students trying to catch a glimpse at the evidence of their favorite teacher's romantic life.

As she stood in the doorway, Mia felt several of them crowding around her, some bumping into her back and hips in their effort to see the flowers. She knew it was time to get them settled down to their math work but she was actually afraid to enter the classroom, afraid of what the flowers meant.

Two other teachers sidled up to Mia, almost as excited as the kids. "Got a new hunk?" one of the other teachers asked with a knowing smile on her face.

The other teacher, older by about ten years, only smirked with cynicism. "Don't get used to it, honey. Just enjoy the flowers now because the men don't continue those sweet little gestures later on. Once they have that ring on your finger, romance goes out the door. Along with a lot of other fun stuff," and she chuckled to herself as she continued walking down the hallway to her own classroom.

Mia shook herself and accepted that she was being silly. The flowers could be from anyone! Besides, the handsome man from the street yesterday wouldn't know where she worked. They'd barely spoken! He didn't even know her name, much less where she worked or even her occupation!

She was being ridiculous and class needed to start. "Okay everyone, settle down and find your seats," she called out, stepping into the room and watching as all of her students crowded in, some of them properly going to their seats but a stubborn group still hovered around her desk, wanting to touch the delicate blossoms.

"To your seats," she called out again, this time with a stern tone of voice. The students heard the authority in her voice this time and followed directions, moving quickly over to their chairs but still looking back at the flowers with longing. The girls were wishing that they had a beau who would send them flowers while the boys were wondering...well, she had no idea what little boys thought of flowers. Probably that they were stinky. She suspected that their opinions wouldn't change as they aged but they would understand the significance to a woman. At least, she hoped that would happen.

"We're going to be learning about..." and she started the class, focusing all of her energy on teaching the kids. It was a challenge though. The pink roses kept catching her eye, distracting her. Just as memories of the man had done all night and all morning. When she walked by her desk, she could smell the delicate scent and the color continuously caught her eye, luring her closer. She resisted the urge as much as she could, but it was a challenge.

By the end of the day, after her last student had gone home, her classroom cleaned up and lessons prepared for the next day, she was exhausted. All she wanted to do was get home, curl up with a cup of tea and watch a movie. Something non-romantic so that she wouldn't even think about the man from the previous night or the way his eyes had shouted out a warning. A warning that her body had certainly understood! Was her body heeding that warning? Absolutely not! Nor had her mind stopped thinking about the note attached to the flowers.

She'd peeked but it hadn't proven anything. All that had been written was, "Beautiful flowers for a beautiful woman." Nothing else, no name, no initials, not even a clue as to who might have sent them to her.

But she knew. She hadn't gotten a name from the mysterious man last night, but she knew the pink roses were from him. She knew it and her heart thundered with that knowledge.

The man didn't play fair, she thought as she pulled her brown coat on, slid her hands into her worn out, leather gloves and grabbed her heavy tote bag filled with papers that she needed to grade tonight. Sending anonymous flowers was cheating, she thought. If she hadn't been so fascinated by the man, she might think that the gesture was a bit creepy. She should probably think it was creepy. After all, there was no note, no name. A little stalkerish.

But her heart throbbed with awareness of the man and his power over her mind even from a distance.

It was time to move on, she told herself firmly. She should throw the flowers away. As her hand fluttered over the light switch to her classroom, she considered doing exactly that. But in the end, the pink roses were simply too beautiful to destroy. And since she was never going to see the man again, what was the point?

She flipped the light switch off and walked out of the building, waving goodbye to the other teachers who were still finishing up in their classrooms.

She headed down the street and turned right onto Rue Sherbrook, pushing harder and making her feet walk faster. She refused to linger over the window displays today even though the weather was nicer, the wind not nearly as sharp as it had been the day before. When she started to approach the store that she loved so much, she slowed and bit her lip. She should...

Instead of going straight, she turned right and headed over to Rue Sainte-Catherine where there were more stores as well as small shops and restaurants. One of her favorite chocolate shops was over on that street as well but she ignored the call of a warm cup of hot chocolate, pushing forward to get home instead. This street reminded her of any other metropolitan city except there were lovely old churches hidden away among the tall buildings. If she'd turned left, she could have lost herself in McGill University, but there were more hills that way as the streets led pedestrians to the Parc du Mont-Royal, the highest point in the city. She was already out of breath from walking so quickly. She didn't need to head uphill and make her trek even worse. All she wanted to do was avoid the man in question and pretend that the stimulating interlude yesterday hadn't happened.

When she finally came to her apartment, which was located in one of the older homes that had been converted to smaller units a few decades ago, she breathed a sigh of relief. And disappointment?

No, she thought as she unlocked her door. That was ridiculous! She wasn't disappointed that she hadn't run into her stranger. Good grief, she'd gone out of her way to make sure that she didn't see the man!

Her apartment was located in one of the older buildings near the Station Place-des-Arts. Every time she walked by the swings with the musical chimes playing, she smiled, thinking how wonderful it would be to bring her own children there one day. The chimes only played when someone swung on the swings so on a Saturday or Sunday afternoon in the spring or fall, it was like a musical heaven as all the swings were filled up with either laughing children or even adults interested in making the chimes ring.

She climbed the stairs to her apartment, wondering what the man was doing tonight. Was he sitting in some elegant restaurant, negotiating a huge deal for whatever company he worked for? Or had he found a sophisticated woman with sexy legs and blond hair, sipping a glass of wine with her? She banished that possibility, not liking the idea of her stranger with a blond woman. Or any woman for that matter.

Flicking on the lights, she came to a full stop for the second time today. She'd gotten one beautiful bouquet of pink roses at her school but...wow! The one bouquet was nothing compared to the sea of pink she was now viewing as she stood just inside the doorway. Her tiny apartment was completely filled with pink roses! They were everywhere! She couldn't even move into her apartment because the hallway was blocked by all of the vases filled with amazingly beautiful blooms. Her apartment smelled better than a perfume counter!

The burst of laughter that escaped her mouth was startling in the silence. She'd dated a few guys in the past. No one could ever call her a player in the dating world, but she'd had a flattering number of invitations.

But no man had ever come close to this. No man had ever done anything so outrageously extravagant.

Carefully, so that she didn't tumble any flower-filled vases over, she set her tote bag down and moved into her apartment, looking around in wonder and awe. Peering into the kitchen, she realized that there was no space on the counters. There were even bouquets of pink roses on top of her fridge. Moving deeper into the apartment, she looked at her bedroom and blushed because, sure enough, there were pink roses on every flat surface and several on the floor. Obviously the delivery person had run out of places to set the vases because there were about twenty of them on the floor of her den area.

This was crazy, she thought, covering her mouth with her hand to stop herself from smiling like a loon.

She wasn't going to question how the man had found out where she lived. That might be a bit too weird. Obviously, he had resources but she hadn't gotten the serial killer or rapist vibe from him last night. Of course, her senses might have been off kilter because of the electricity she'd felt coming from his light touch, but she was going with her gut on this man. He was dangerous, but not in the normal criminal manner.

When the doorbell rang, she knew exactly who it was. She didn't even consider not opening the door this time. Of course, having a huge number of roses delivered to one's house did not make the man un-dangerous. Not in any way. But there was just something about the gesture that called to her. She wanted to see him, wanted to understand what kind of man would do something so crazy.

Sure enough, as soon as she opened the door, her eyes looked upwards to find the man's dark eyes looking down at her.

"Vous etes un fou," she told him without thinking. She couldn't wipe the silly grin from her features even as she called him a fool in French.

One dark eyebrow went up in reaction. "Excuse me?" he prompted and leaned forward, handing her a single pink rose.

She blinked and realized that she'd spoken in French instead of English and shook her head. "Sorry. I said you're a fool, sir."

His eyes lightened and she felt the temperature in the apartment increase by about twenty degrees. "Ah, you speak French when you're flustered." He moved closer. "I think I like that about you. Very sexy."

Mia realized she was holding her breath and filled her lungs. Unfortunately, the air was filled with his scent which was spicy and inviting and oh-so-alluring. "What are you doing here?"

He smiled slightly. "I came to see if you'd gotten my message."

Her eyes laughed even though she wouldn't allow herself to do the same. She felt a girlish giggle starting to bubble up but she tamped it down mercilessly. "That you're insane?" she asked, gesturing behind her at all of the flowers. Everywhere!

His deep chuckle did something deep inside of her. Something sinful and sexy and her body wanted to just curl up around this man and his scent as well as that shocking laughter.

"That I would like to take you out to dinner tonight."

She pulled back, surprised that he looked serious. "Really?"

His hands moved up to turn her ever so slightly towards the banquet of roses. "It was in the note."

She was confused and looked back up at him. "The note?" Why couldn't she stop staring at him? He was a devastatingly handsome man, but that shouldn't mean anything to her. She should be looking inward, towards who he was as a person. Was she truly so superficial?

"There was a note," he confirmed, nodding his head slightly.

She sighed. "You've got to be kidding, right? I just got home and saw all of this. There's no way I would be able to find a note in this gesture."

Ramzi watched the beautiful woman carefully, enjoying the way she blushed when he moved closer, sighed when he stepped slightly away from her and lowered those long, dark lashes when she tried to hide both reactions from him. She was right here with him, her attraction just as strong as what he was feeling towards her.

For the first time, he looked in at her apartment and noticed the sea of pink. He'd been so intent on watching her animated features that he hadn't noticed the insane number of flowers. Her apartment was indeed filled to the brim with flowers. "I didn't realize that your home was so small," he explained with another deep chuckle. He stepped past her and glanced around. When he found what he was looking for, he lifted the small, white envelope out of the bouquet and handed it to her.

"I believe this will explain."

Mia's eyes filled with amusement but she accepted the envelope, pulling out the card. "Dinner tonight. Seven o'clock."

"That's all?" she asked, laughing softly at the note that was more of a command than a request for a date. "It wasn't even a question, sir. And no, I don't know your name so there's no possibility of me going out to dinner with you."

He leaned forward, backing her against the wall. "Pasta covered in cheese and sauce, maybe some seafood mixed in with lots of garlic, bread with real butter," he said the words softly, as if they were a caress and she felt them all the way down to her toes.

"Real butter?" she whispered, her eyes dropping to his lips. "I don't eat real butter," she replied.

His hand came up, a long finger sliding down her cheek to caress her and to appease his curiosity at what she would feel like. "Tonight, live on the wild side and have real butter. And chocolate dessert with extra cream and top off the evening with…" he almost said "me" but held back, instinctively knowing that he'd have to move slower with this woman, "the most excellent brandy you've ever tasted."

Mia unconsciously licked her lips and sighed. "I can't imagine the most excellent brandy," she replied back, falling under his spell even though she knew she should kick him out and run as far away from him as she could.

His smile grew with her words. "Then I shall have to teach you about the fabulous world of brandy."

"Brandy," she whispered, sensing he was coming closer but her mind couldn't focus on his proximity. Only his mouth and his incredible, masculine smell that was now surrounding her. Brandy might be nice, but this man's scent was the most potent aphrodisiac she'd ever experienced.

"Among other things," he returned.

Mia shivered at the idea of "other things". She wanted to know what he might be referring to, but her lips couldn't form the words. A part of her was too afraid of those "other things". She knew she should not want those "other things".

But she did! Oh, goodness, she wanted those "other things" with this man so badly, she could almost taste them! In less than twenty-four hours and with only a smattering of conversation between them, she was almost panting after this man with a scandalous lack of decorum.

If you enjoyed this excerpt, look for Pregnant with the Sheik's Baby at your favorite e-book retailer. It's available for preorder now! Also look for the free series introduction stories on ElizabethLennox.com!

List of Elizabeth Lennox Books

The Texas Tycoon's Temptation

The Royal Cordova Trilogy
Escaping a Royal Wedding
The Man's Outrageous Demands
Mistress to the Prince

The Attracelli Family Series
Never Dare a Tycoon
Falling For the Boss
Risky Negotiations
Proposal to Love
Love's Not Terrifying
Romantic Acquisition

The Billionaire's Terms: Prison or Passion
The Sheik's Love Child
The Sheik's Unfinished Business
The Greek Tycoon's Lover
The Sheik's Sensuous Trap
The Greek's Baby Bargain
The Italian's Bedroom Deal
The Billionaire's Gamble
The Tycoon's Seduction Plan
The Sheik's Rebellious Mistress
The Sheik's Missing Bride
Blackmailed by the Billionaire
The Billionaire's Runaway Bride
The Billionaire's Elusive Lover
The Intimate, Intricate Rescue

The Sisterhood Trilogy
The Sheik's Virgin Lover
The Billionaire's Impulsive Lover
The Russian's Tender Lover
The Billionaire's Gentle Rescue

The Tycoon's Toddler Surprise
The Tycoon's Tender Triumph

The Friends Forever Series
The Sheik's Mysterious Mistress
The Duke's Willful Wife
The Tycoon's Marriage Exchange

The Sheik's Secret Twins
The Russian's Furious Fiancée
The Tycoon's Misunderstood Bride

Love By Accident Series
The Sheik's Pregnant Lover
The Sheik's Furious Bride
The Duke's Runaway Princess

The Russian's Pregnant Mistress

The Lovers Exchange Series
The Earl's Outrageous Lover
The Tycoon's Resistant Lover

The Sheik's Reluctant Lover
The Spanish Tycoon's Temptress

The Berutelli Escape
Resisting The Tycoon's Seduction
The Billionaire's Secretive Enchantress

The Big Apple Brotherhood
The Billionaire's Pregnant Lover
The Sheik's Rediscovered Lover

The Tycoon's Defiant Southern Belle

The Sheik's Dangerous Lover (Novella)

The Thorpe Brothers
His Captive Lover
His Unexpected Lover
His Secretive Lover
His Challenging Lover

The Sheik's Defiant Fiancée (Novella)
The Prince's Resistant Lover (Novella)
The Tycoon's Make-Believe Fiancée (Novella)

The Friendship Series
The Billionaire's Masquerade
The Russian's Dangerous Game
The Sheik's Beautiful Intruder

The Love and Danger Series – Romantic Mysteries
Intimate Desires
Intimate Caresses
Intimate Secrets
Intimate Whispers

The Alfieri Saga
The Italian's Passionate Return (Novella)
Her Gentle Capture
His Reluctant Lover
Her Unexpected Admirer
Her Tender Tyrant
Releasing the Billionaire's Passion (Novella)
His Expectant Lover

The Sheik's Intimate Proposition (Novella)

The Hart Sisters Trilogy
The Billionaire's Secret Marriage
The Italian's Twin Surprise (USA Today™ Best Seller!)
The Forbidden Russian Lover (USA Today™ Best Seller!)

The War, Love, and Harmony Series
Fighting with the Infuriating Prince (Novella)
Dancing with the Dangerous Prince (Novella)
The Sheik's Secret Bride
The Sheik's Angry Bride
The Sheik's Blackmailed Bride
The Sheik's Convenient Bride

The Boarding School Series
The Boarding School Series Introduction
The Greek's Forgotten Wife
The Duke's Blackmailed Bride
The Russian's Runaway Bride
The Sheik's Baby Surprise
The Tycoon's Captured Heart
His Unexpected Protégé (Novella)

The Samara Royal Family Series – February 2016 to June 2016
The Samara Royal Family Series Introduction
Pregnant with the Sheik's Baby
The Prince's Intimate Abduction
The Prince's Forbidden Lover
The Sheik's Captured Princess
The Sheik's Jealous Princess

Made in the USA
Monee, IL
17 September 2022

14189928R00066